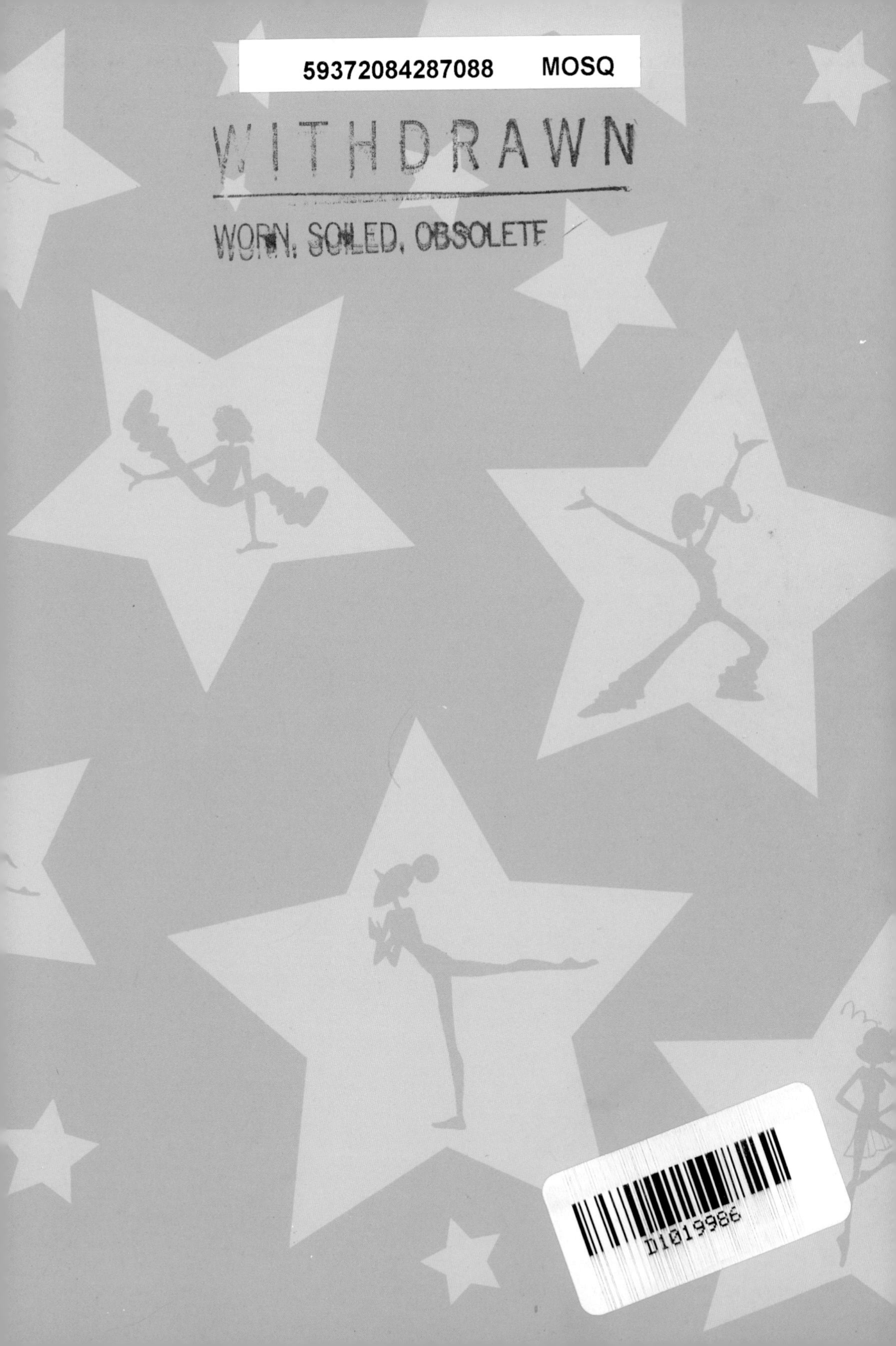

Dance Class

Crip • Art

Béka • Story

Maëla Cosson • Color

PAPERCUT™

New York

Dance Class Graphic Novels Available from PAPERCUTZ™

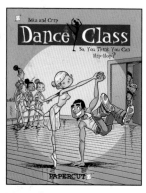

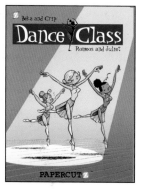

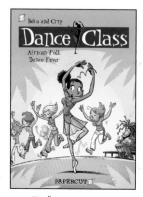

#1 "So, You Think
You Can Hip-Hop?"

#2 "Romeos and Juliet"

#3 "African Folk
Dance Fever"

Coming Soon!

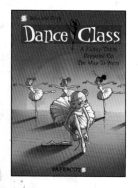

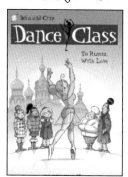

#4 "A Funny Thing Happened
on the Way to Paris..."

#5 "To Russia,
With Love"

DANCE CLASS #4
"A Funny Thing Happened
on the Way to Paris..."
Studio Danse [Dance Class], by Béka & Crip
© 2010 BAMBOO ÉDITION.
www.bamboo.fr

Béka - Writer
Crip - Artist
Maëla Cosson - Colorist
Joe Johnson - Translation
Tom Orzechowski - Lettering
Grace Ilori - Production
Michael Petranek - Associate Editor
Jim Salicrup
Editor-in-Chief

ISBN: 978-1-59707-384-4

Printed in China
March 2013 by New Era Printing Ltd.
Unit C. 8/F Worldwide Centre
123 Chung Tau, Kowloon
Hong Kong

Distributed by Macmillan
First Papercutz Printing

DANCE CLASS graphic novels are available for $10.99 only in hardcover. Available from booksellers everywhere. You can also order online from www.papercutz.com. Or call 1-800-886-1223, Monday through Fridays, 9 - 5 EST. MC, Visa, and AmEx accepted. To order by mail, please add $4.00 for postage and handling for first book ordered, $1.00 for each additional book and make check payable to NBM Publishing. Send to: Papercutz, 160 Broadway, Suite 700, East Wing, New York, NY 10038.

DANCE CLASS graphic novels are also available digitally wherever e-books are sold

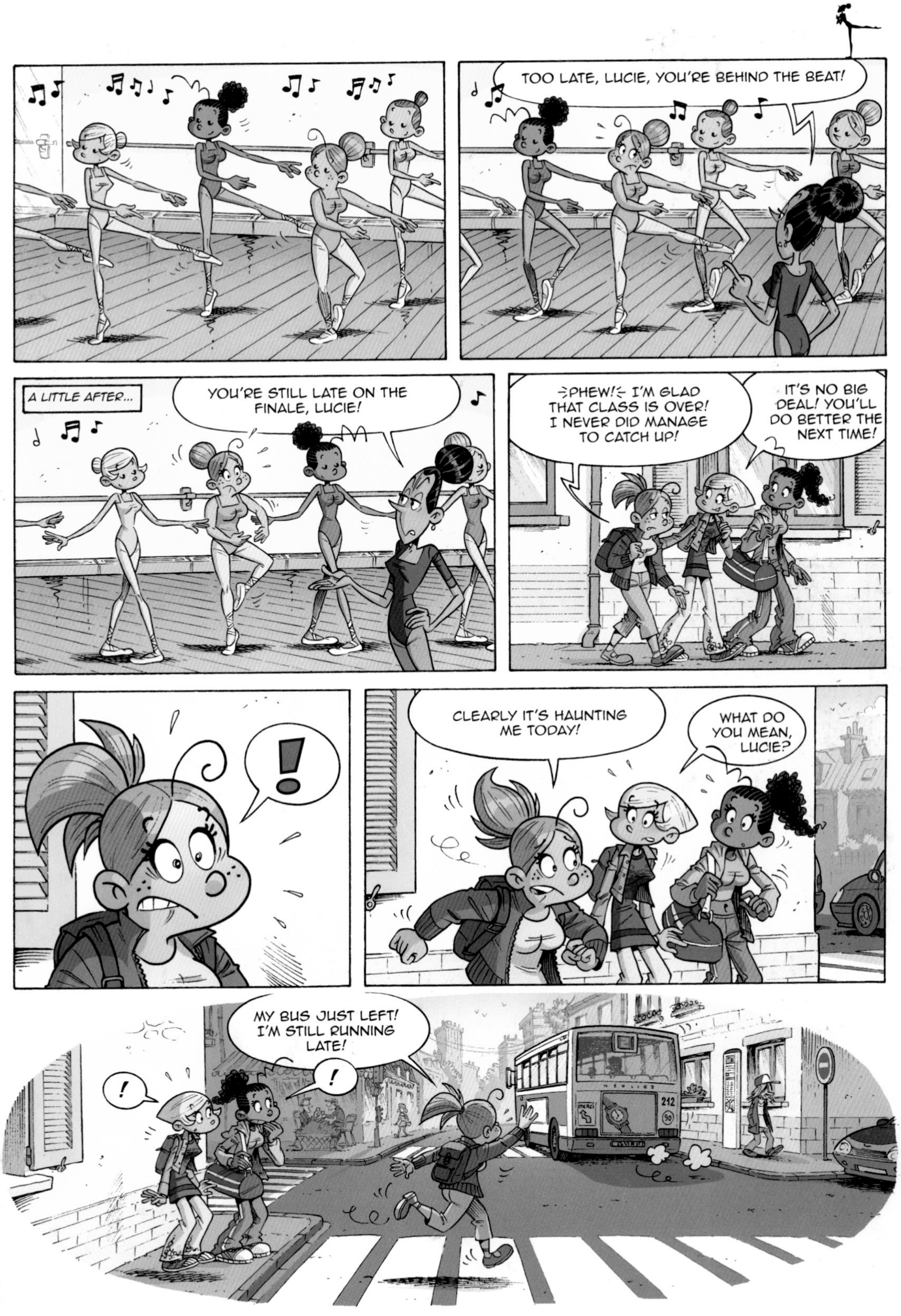
TOO LATE, LUCIE, YOU'RE BEHIND THE BEAT!
A LITTLE AFTER...
YOU'RE STILL LATE ON THE FINALE, LUCIE!
PHEW! I'M GLAD THAT CLASS IS OVER! I NEVER DID MANAGE TO CATCH UP!
IT'S NO BIG DEAL! YOU'LL DO BETTER THE NEXT TIME!
!
CLEARLY IT'S HAUNTING ME TODAY!
WHAT DO YOU MEAN, LUCIE?
!
MY BUS JUST LEFT! I'M STILL RUNNING LATE!
!
212

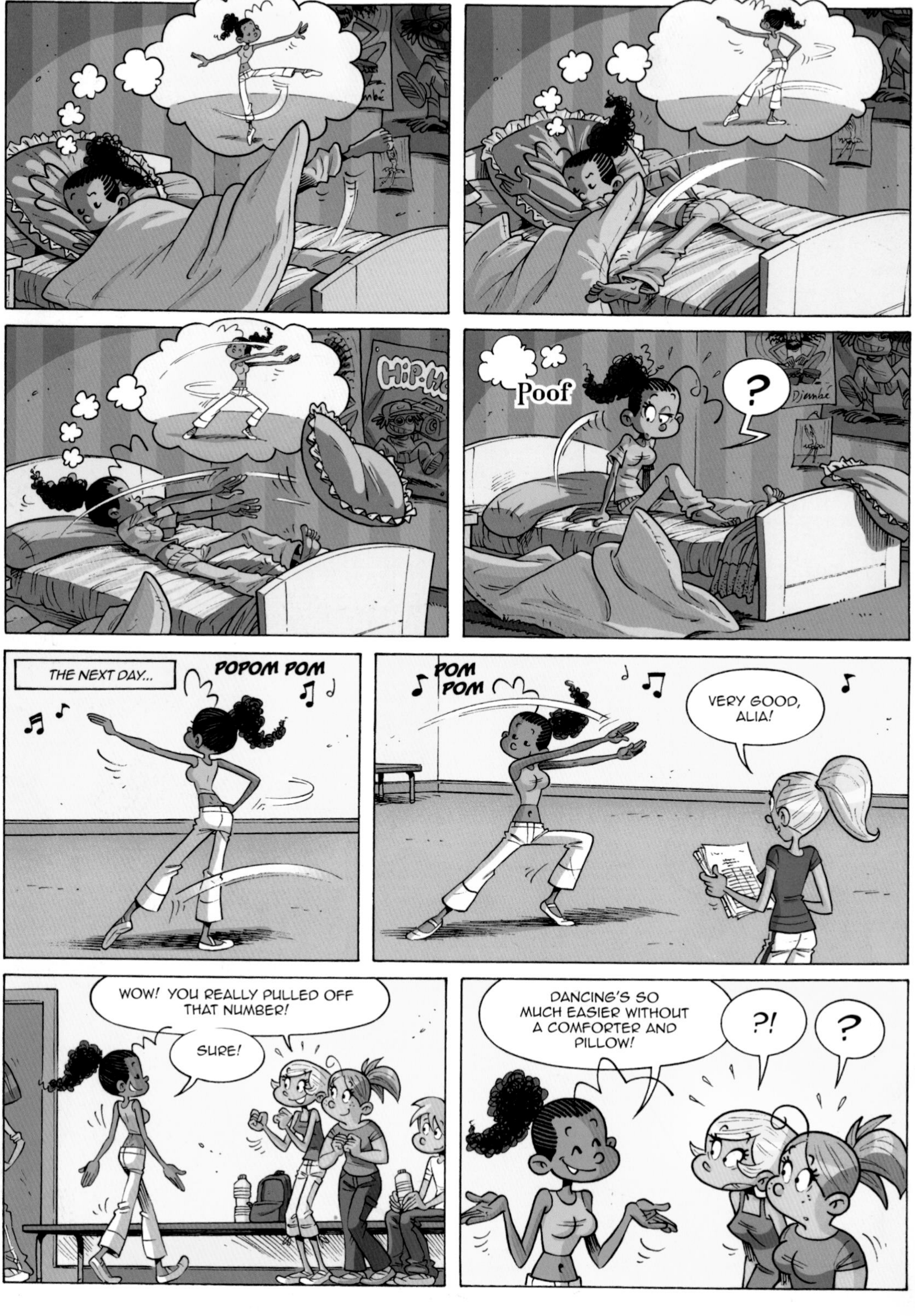
Poof
?
THE NEXT DAY...
POPOM POM
POM POM
VERY GOOD, ALIA!
WOW! YOU REALLY PULLED OFF THAT NUMBER!
SURE!
DANCING'S SO MUCH EASIER WITHOUT A COMFORTER AND PILLOW!
?!
?

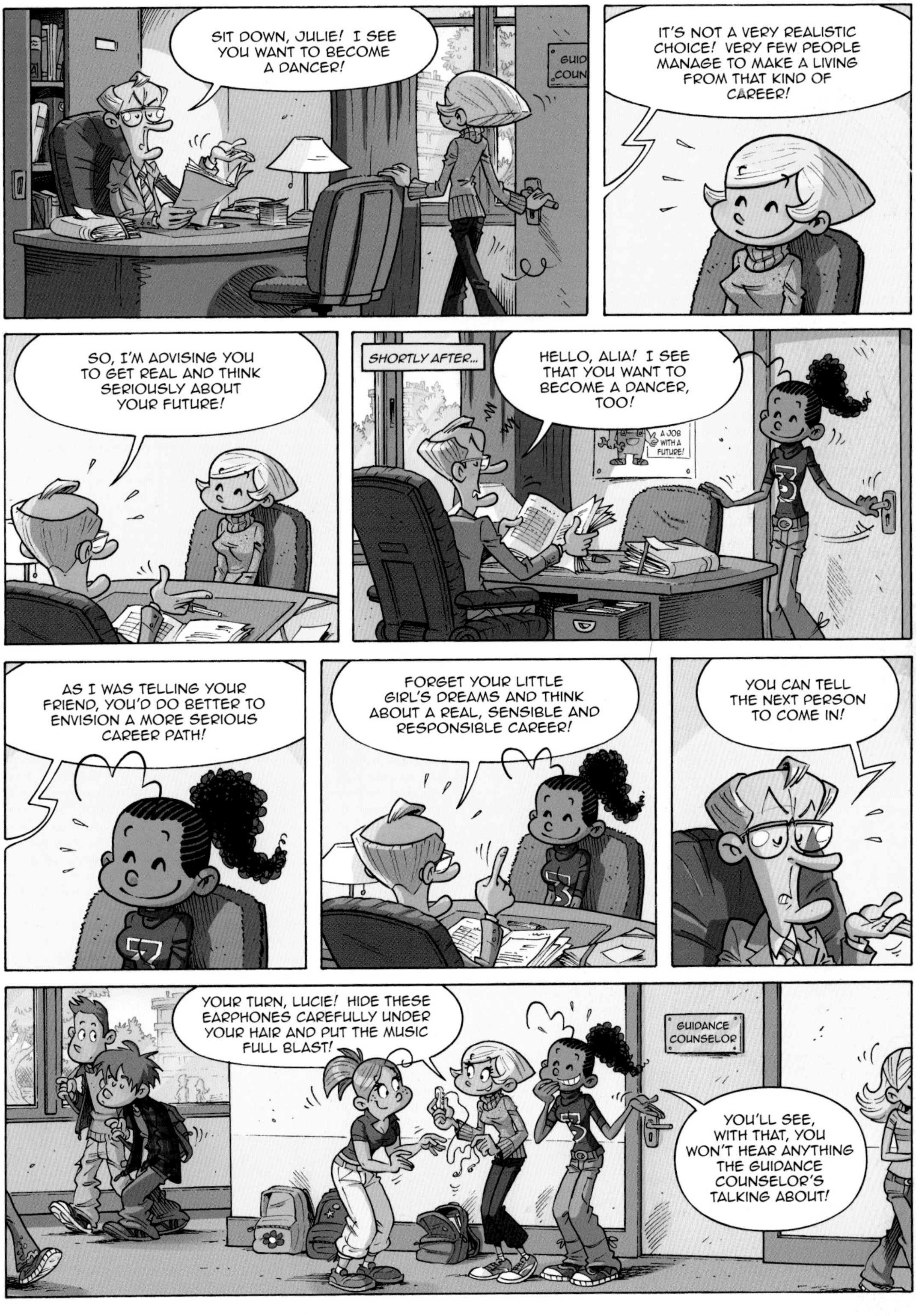
SIT DOWN, JULIE! I SEE YOU WANT TO BECOME A DANCER!
GUID COUN
IT'S NOT A VERY REALISTIC CHOICE! VERY FEW PEOPLE MANAGE TO MAKE A LIVING FROM THAT KIND OF CAREER!
SO, I'M ADVISING YOU TO GET REAL AND THINK SERIOUSLY ABOUT YOUR FUTURE!
SHORTLY AFTER...
HELLO, ALIA! I SEE THAT YOU WANT TO BECOME A DANCER, TOO!
A JOB WITH A FUTURE!
AS I WAS TELLING YOUR FRIEND, YOU'D DO BETTER TO ENVISION A MORE SERIOUS CAREER PATH!
FORGET YOUR LITTLE GIRL'S DREAMS AND THINK ABOUT A REAL, SENSIBLE AND RESPONSIBLE CAREER!
YOU CAN TELL THE NEXT PERSON TO COME IN!
YOUR TURN, LUCIE! HIDE THESE EARPHONES CAREFULLY UNDER YOUR HAIR AND PUT THE MUSIC FULL BLAST!
GUIDANCE COUNSELOR
YOU'LL SEE, WITH THAT, YOU WON'T HEAR ANYTHING THE GUIDANCE COUNSELOR'S TALKING ABOUT!

HI, LUCIE!

HELLO, MA'AM!

HELLO.

THE PARTY AT YOUR DAD'S LAST SATURDAY WAS AWESOME! WE HAD SO MUCH FUN!

YES! EVERY-BODY LOVED IT!

!!

WHAT?! YOU HAD A PARTY AT YOUR DAD'S?

NO WAY! THIS ISN'T HOW THINGS ARE GOING TO GO, BELIEVE YOU ME!

NEXT SATURDAY, YOU'LL ALL COME TO MY HOUSE! AND DON'T FORGET TO TELL YOUR FRIENDS!

I'LL SHOW YOU WHAT A REAL PARTY IS!

HEE HEE! OUR PLAN WORKED!

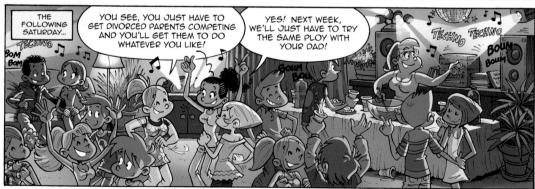

THE FOLLOWING SATURDAY...

YOU SEE, YOU JUST HAVE TO GET DIVORCED PARENTS COMPETING AND YOU'LL GET THEM TO DO WHATEVER YOU LIKE!

YES! NEXT WEEK, WE'LL JUST HAVE TO TRY THE SAME PLOY WITH YOUR DAD!

TECHNO

BOM BOM

BOUM BOM

BOUM BOM

TECHNO TECHNO

BOUM BOM

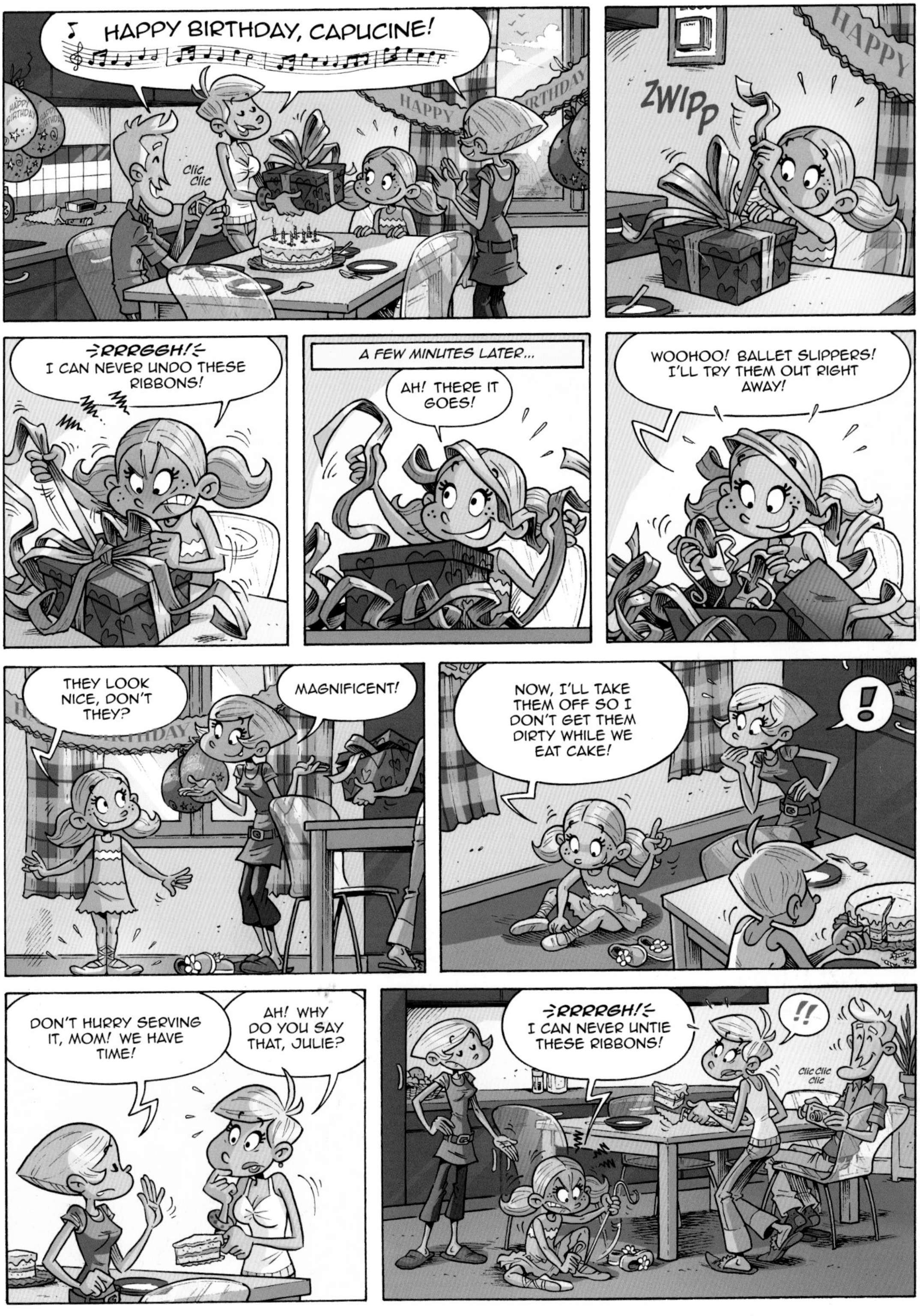
HAPPY BIRTHDAY, CAPUCINE!
Clic Clic
HAPPY BIRTHDAY
ZWIPP
HAPPY
RRRGGH! I CAN NEVER UNDO THESE RIBBONS!
A FEW MINUTES LATER...
AH! THERE IT GOES!
WOOHOO! BALLET SLIPPERS! I'LL TRY THEM OUT RIGHT AWAY!
THEY LOOK NICE, DON'T THEY?
MAGNIFICENT!
NOW, I'LL TAKE THEM OFF SO I DON'T GET THEM DIRTY WHILE WE EAT CAKE!
!
DON'T HURRY SERVING IT, MOM! WE HAVE TIME!
AH! WHY DO YOU SAY THAT, JULIE?
RRRRGH! I CAN NEVER UNTIE THESE RIBBONS!
!!
Clic Clic Clic

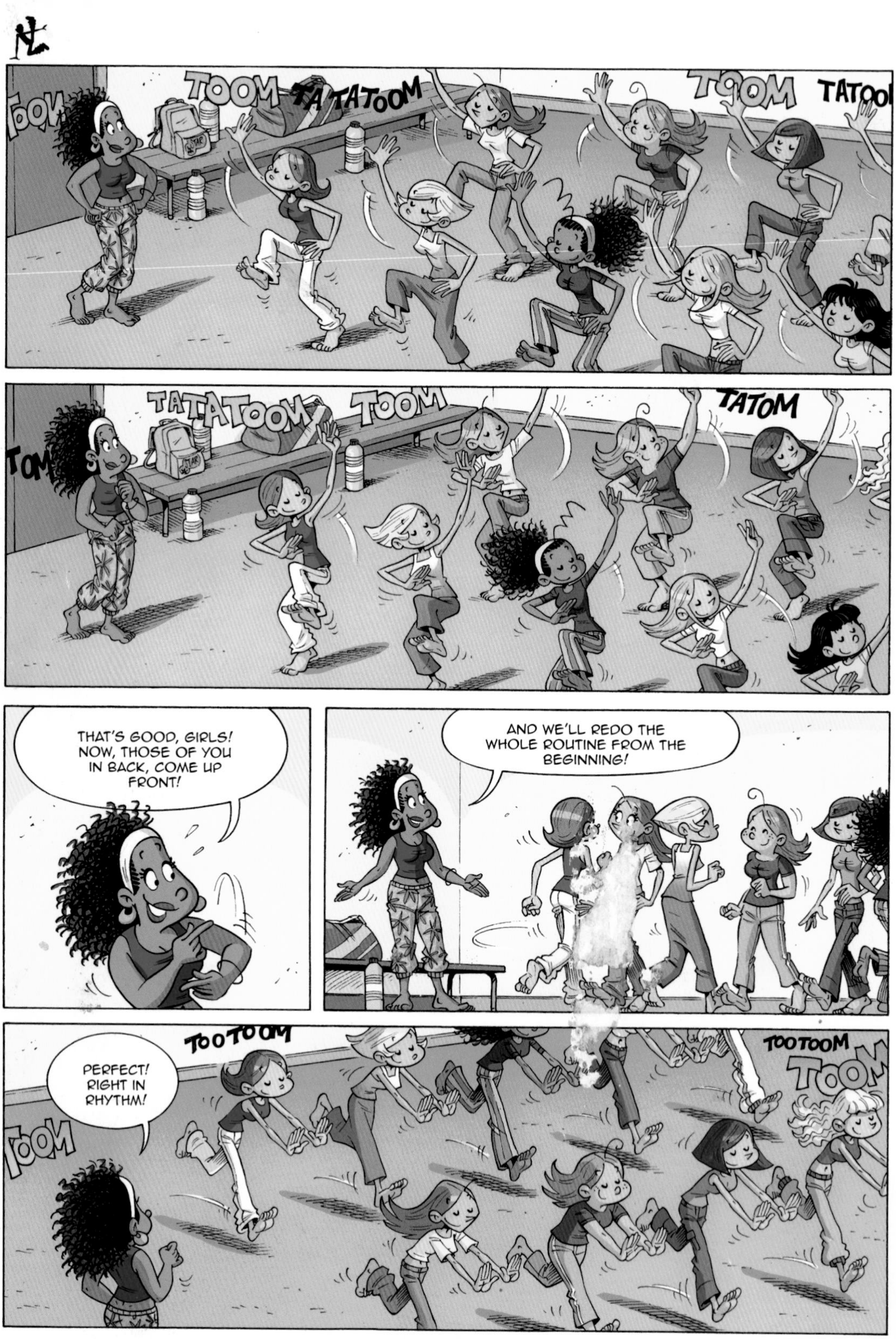
TOOM
TOOM
TA TATOOM
TOOM
TATOO
TOM
TATATOOM
TOOM
TATOM
THAT'S GOOD, GIRLS! NOW, THOSE OF YOU IN BACK, COME UP FRONT!
AND WE'LL REDO THE WHOLE ROUTINE FROM THE BEGINNING!
TOOTOOM
PERFECT! RIGHT IN RHYTHM!
TOOM
TOOTOOM
TOOM

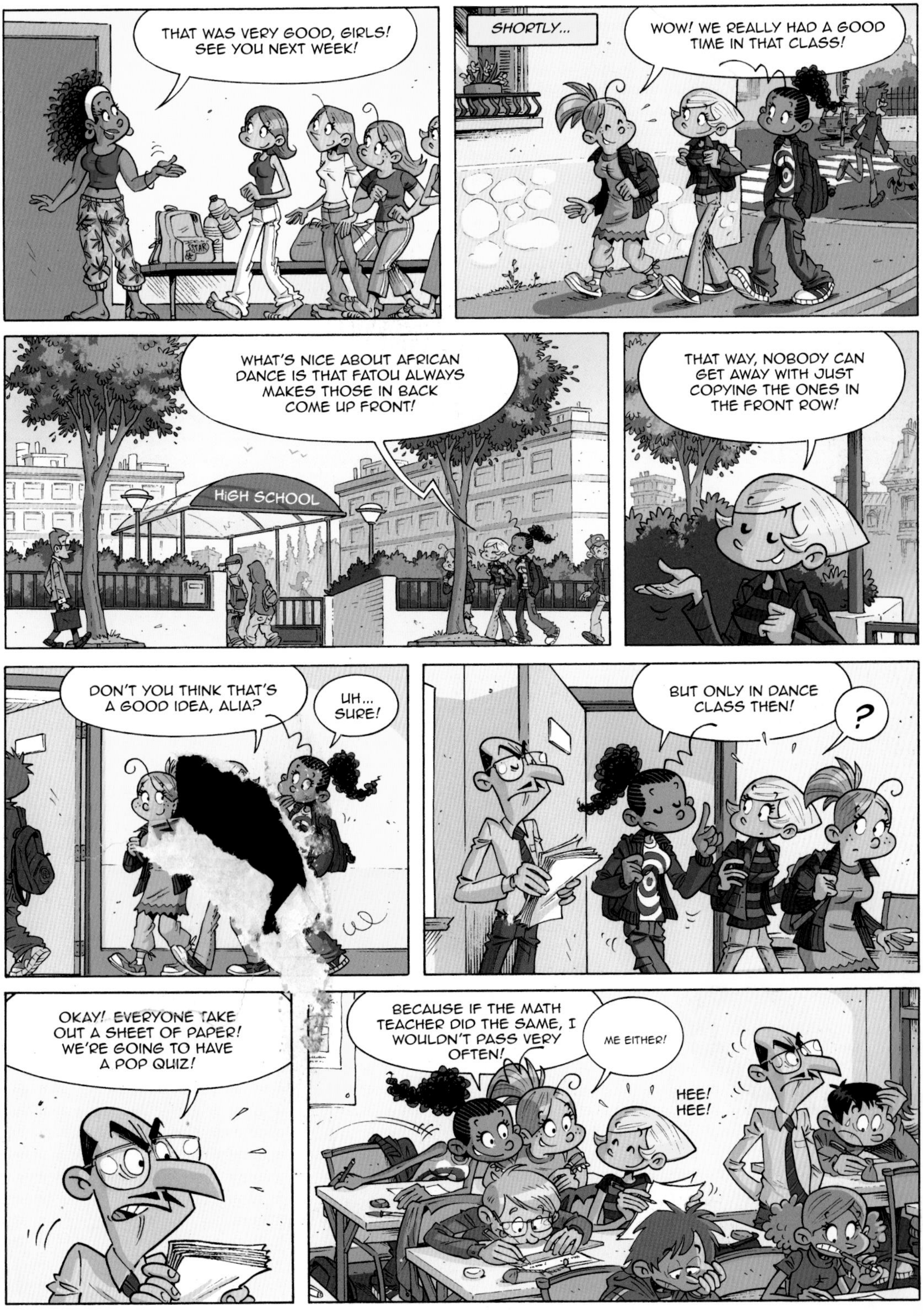
THAT WAS VERY GOOD, GIRLS! SEE YOU NEXT WEEK!
SHORTLY...
WOW! WE REALLY HAD A GOOD TIME IN THAT CLASS!
WHAT'S NICE ABOUT AFRICAN DANCE IS THAT FATOU ALWAYS MAKES THOSE IN BACK COME UP FRONT!
HIGH SCHOOL
THAT WAY, NOBODY CAN GET AWAY WITH JUST COPYING THE ONES IN THE FRONT ROW!
DON'T YOU THINK THAT'S A GOOD IDEA, ALIA?
UH... SURE!
BUT ONLY IN DANCE CLASS THEN!
?
OKAY! EVERYONE TAKE OUT A SHEET OF PAPER! WE'RE GOING TO HAVE A POP QUIZ!
BECAUSE IF THE MATH TEACHER DID THE SAME, I WOULDN'T PASS VERY OFTEN!
ME EITHER!
HEE! HEE!

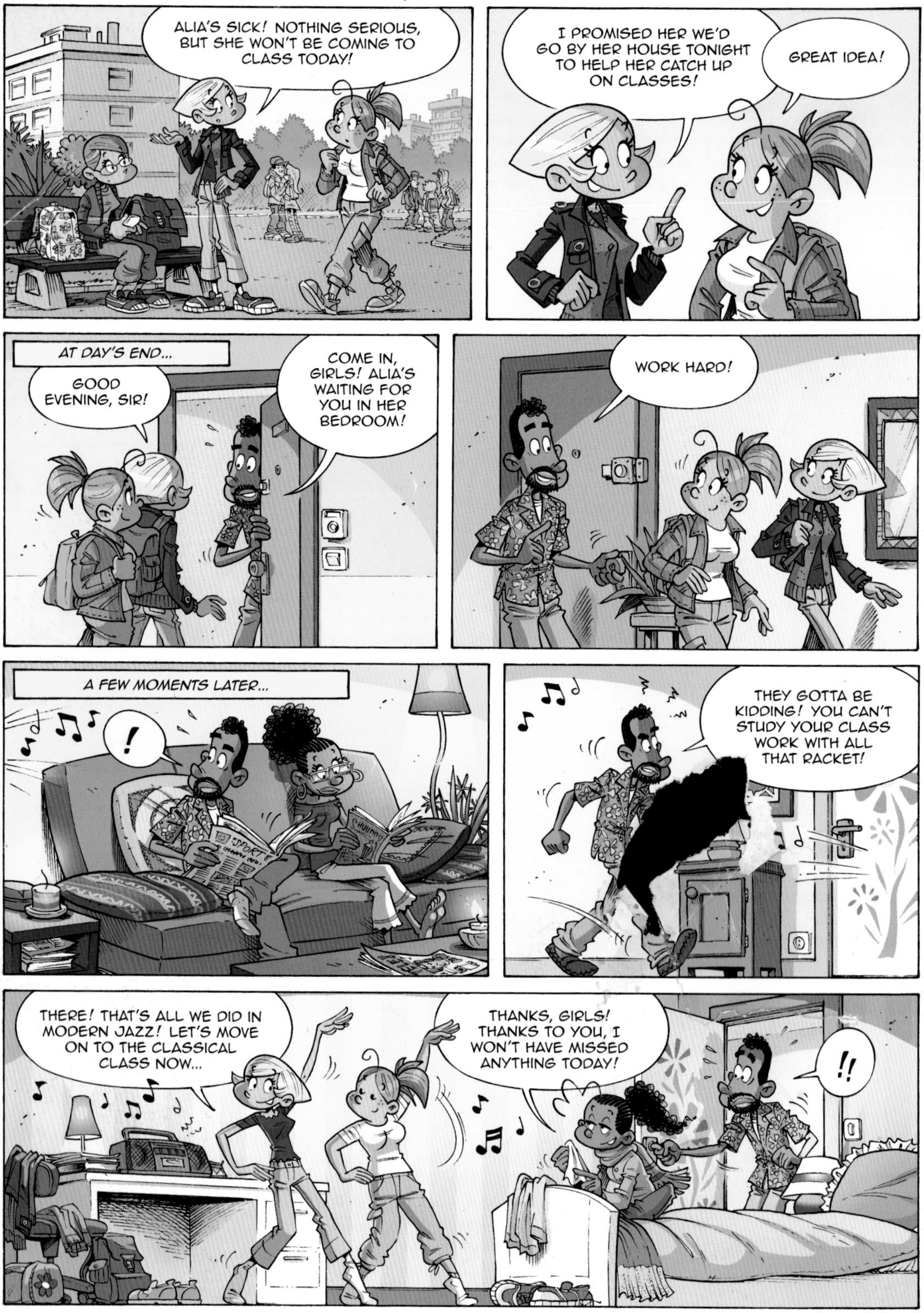
ALIA'S SICK! NOTHING SERIOUS, BUT SHE WON'T BE COMING TO CLASS TODAY!
I PROMISED HER WE'D GO BY HER HOUSE TONIGHT TO HELP HER CATCH UP ON CLASSES!
GREAT IDEA!
AT DAY'S END...
GOOD EVENING, SIR!
COME IN, GIRLS! ALIA'S WAITING FOR YOU IN HER BEDROOM!
WORK HARD!
A FEW MOMENTS LATER...
!
THEY GOTTA BE KIDDING! YOU CAN'T STUDY YOUR CLASS WORK WITH ALL THAT RACKET!
THERE! THAT'S ALL WE DID IN MODERN JAZZ! LET'S MOVE ON TO THE CLASSICAL CLASS NOW...
THANKS, GIRLS! THANKS TO YOU, I WON'T HAVE MISSED ANYTHING TODAY!
!!

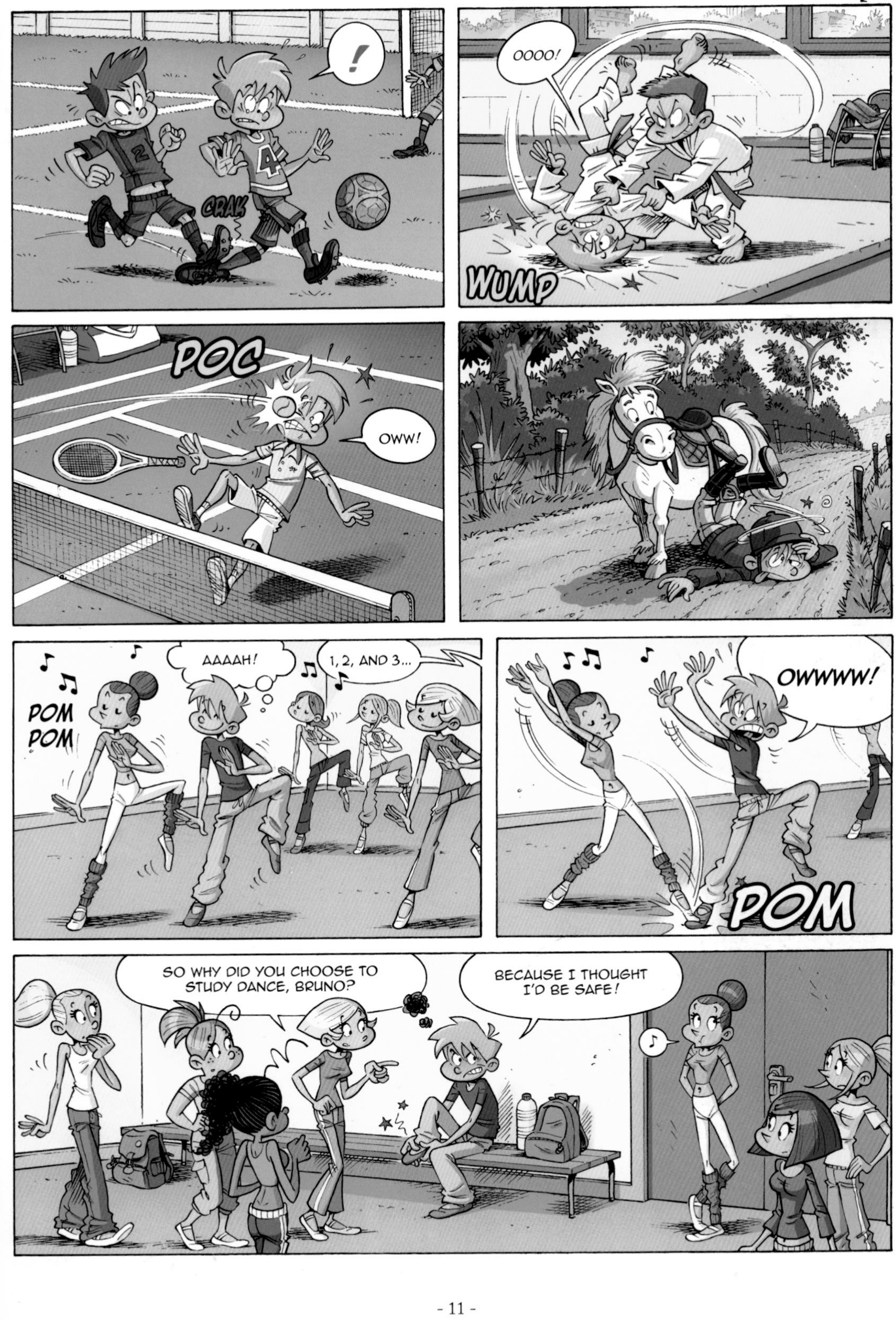
!
CRAK
OOOO!
WUMP
POC
OWW!
POM
POM
AAAAH!
1, 2, AND 3...
OWWWW!
POM
SO WHY DID YOU CHOOSE TO STUDY DANCE, BRUNO?
BECAUSE I THOUGHT I'D BE SAFE!

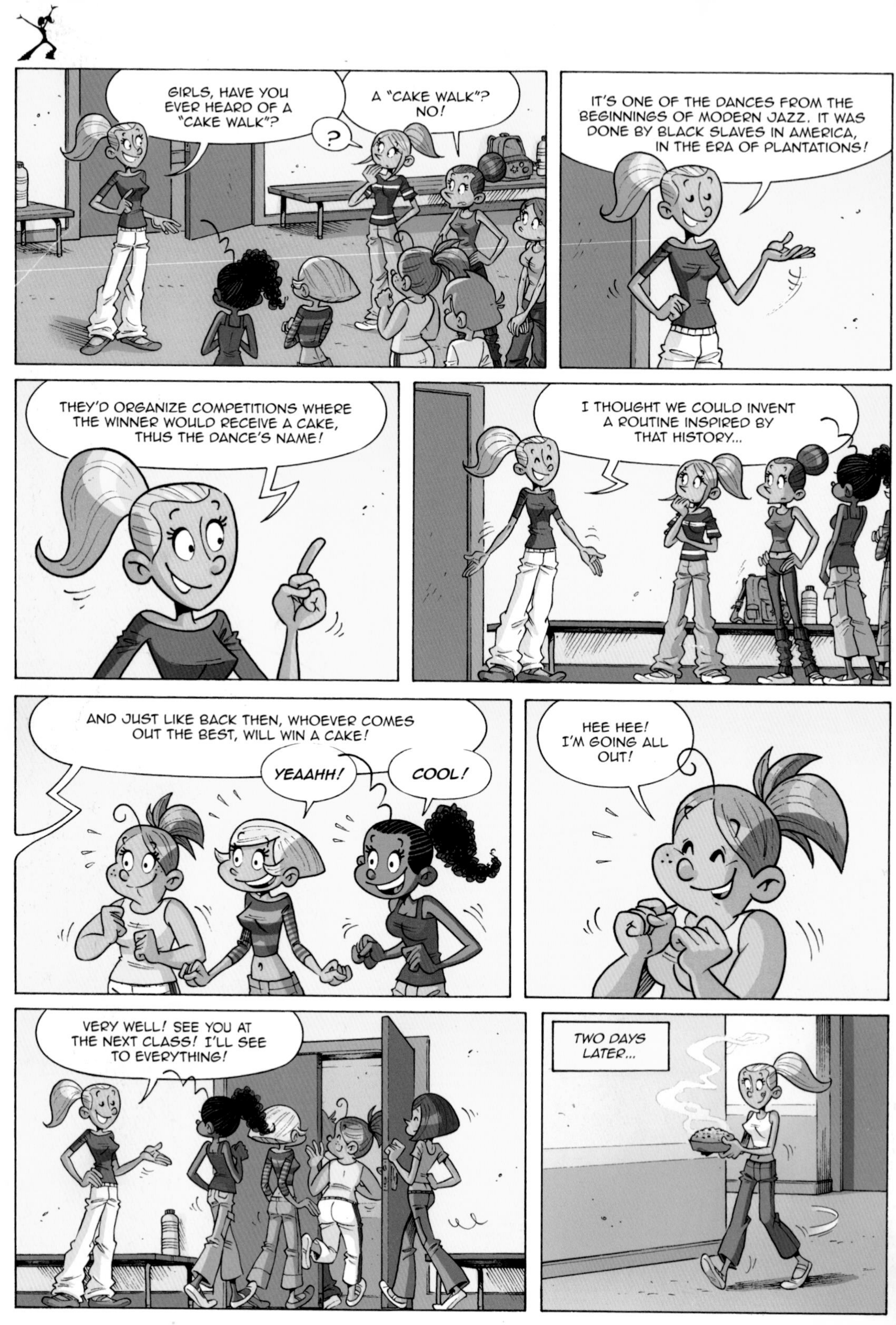
GIRLS, HAVE YOU EVER HEARD OF A "CAKE WALK"?
?
A "CAKE WALK"? NO!
IT'S ONE OF THE DANCES FROM THE BEGINNINGS OF MODERN JAZZ. IT WAS DONE BY BLACK SLAVES IN AMERICA, IN THE ERA OF PLANTATIONS!
THEY'D ORGANIZE COMPETITIONS WHERE THE WINNER WOULD RECEIVE A CAKE, THUS THE DANCE'S NAME!
I THOUGHT WE COULD INVENT A ROUTINE INSPIRED BY THAT HISTORY...
AND JUST LIKE BACK THEN, WHOEVER COMES OUT THE BEST, WILL WIN A CAKE!
YEAAHH!
COOL!
HEE HEE! I'M GOING ALL OUT!
VERY WELL! SEE YOU AT THE NEXT CLASS! I'LL SEE TO EVERYTHING!
TWO DAYS LATER...

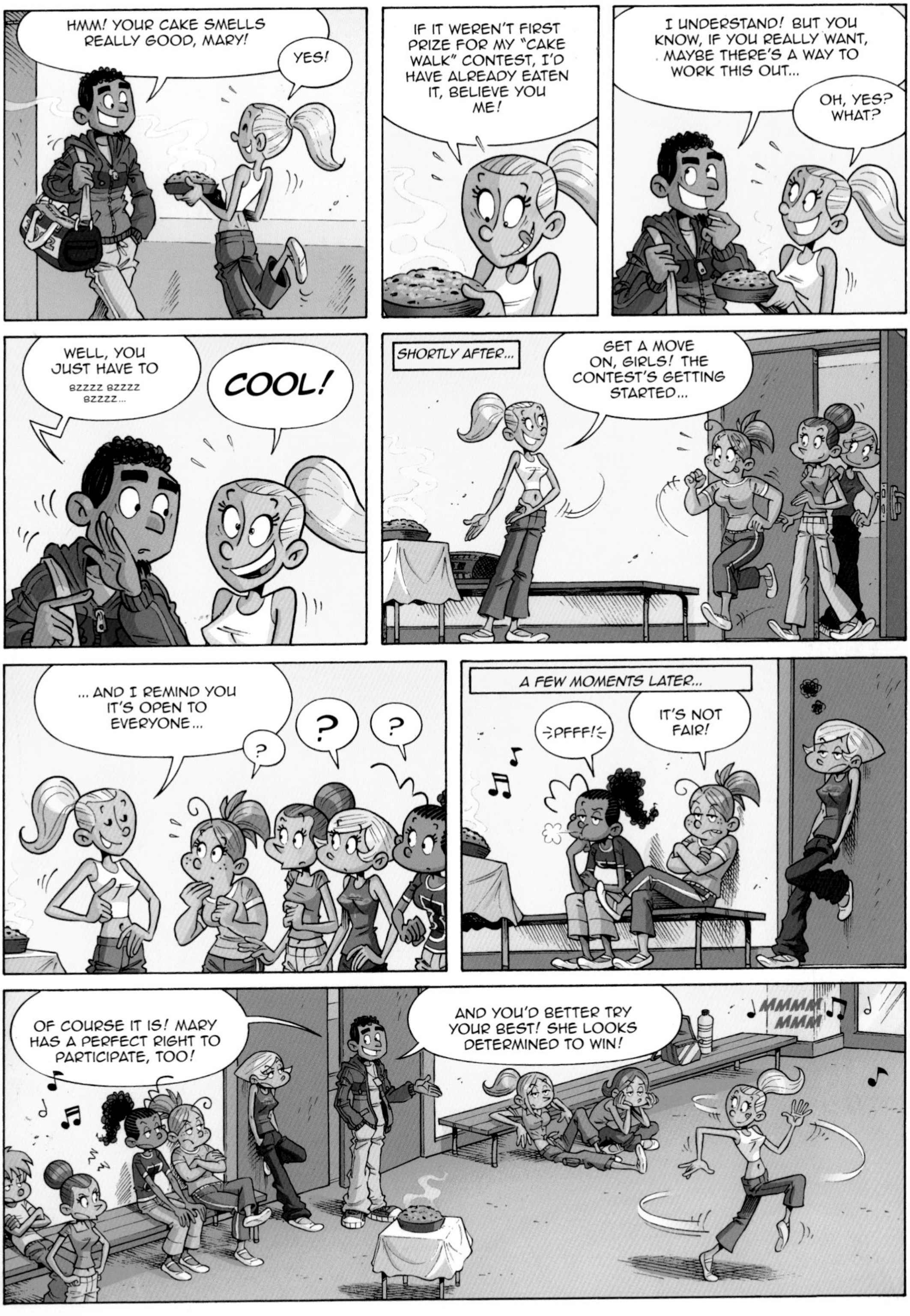
HMM! YOUR CAKE SMELLS REALLY GOOD, MARY!
YES!
IF IT WEREN'T FIRST PRIZE FOR MY "CAKE WALK" CONTEST, I'D HAVE ALREADY EATEN IT, BELIEVE YOU ME!
I UNDERSTAND! BUT YOU KNOW, IF YOU REALLY WANT, MAYBE THERE'S A WAY TO WORK THIS OUT...
OH, YES? WHAT?
WELL, YOU JUST HAVE TO
BZZZZ BZZZZ BZZZZ...
COOL!
SHORTLY AFTER...
GET A MOVE ON, GIRLS! THE CONTEST'S GETTING STARTED...
... AND I REMIND YOU IT'S OPEN TO EVERYONE...
?
?
?
A FEW MOMENTS LATER...
PFFF!
IT'S NOT FAIR!
OF COURSE IT IS! MARY HAS A PERFECT RIGHT TO PARTICIPATE, TOO!
AND YOU'D BETTER TRY YOUR BEST! SHE LOOKS DETERMINED TO WIN!
MMMM MMM

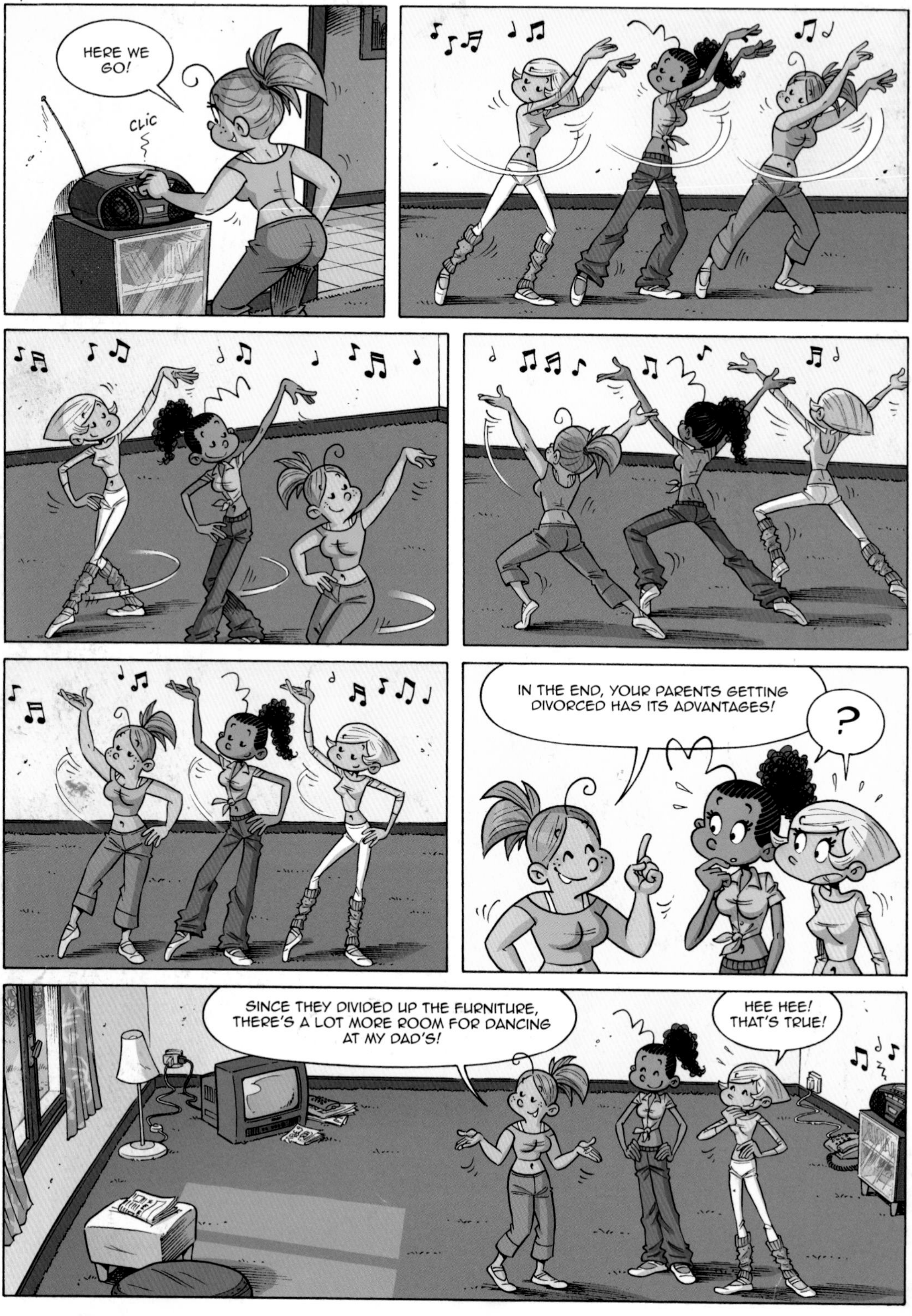
HERE WE GO!
CLIC
IN THE END, YOUR PARENTS GETTING DIVORCED HAS ITS ADVANTAGES!
?
SINCE THEY DIVIDED UP THE FURNITURE, THERE'S A LOT MORE ROOM FOR DANCING AT MY DAD'S!
HEE HEE! THAT'S TRUE!

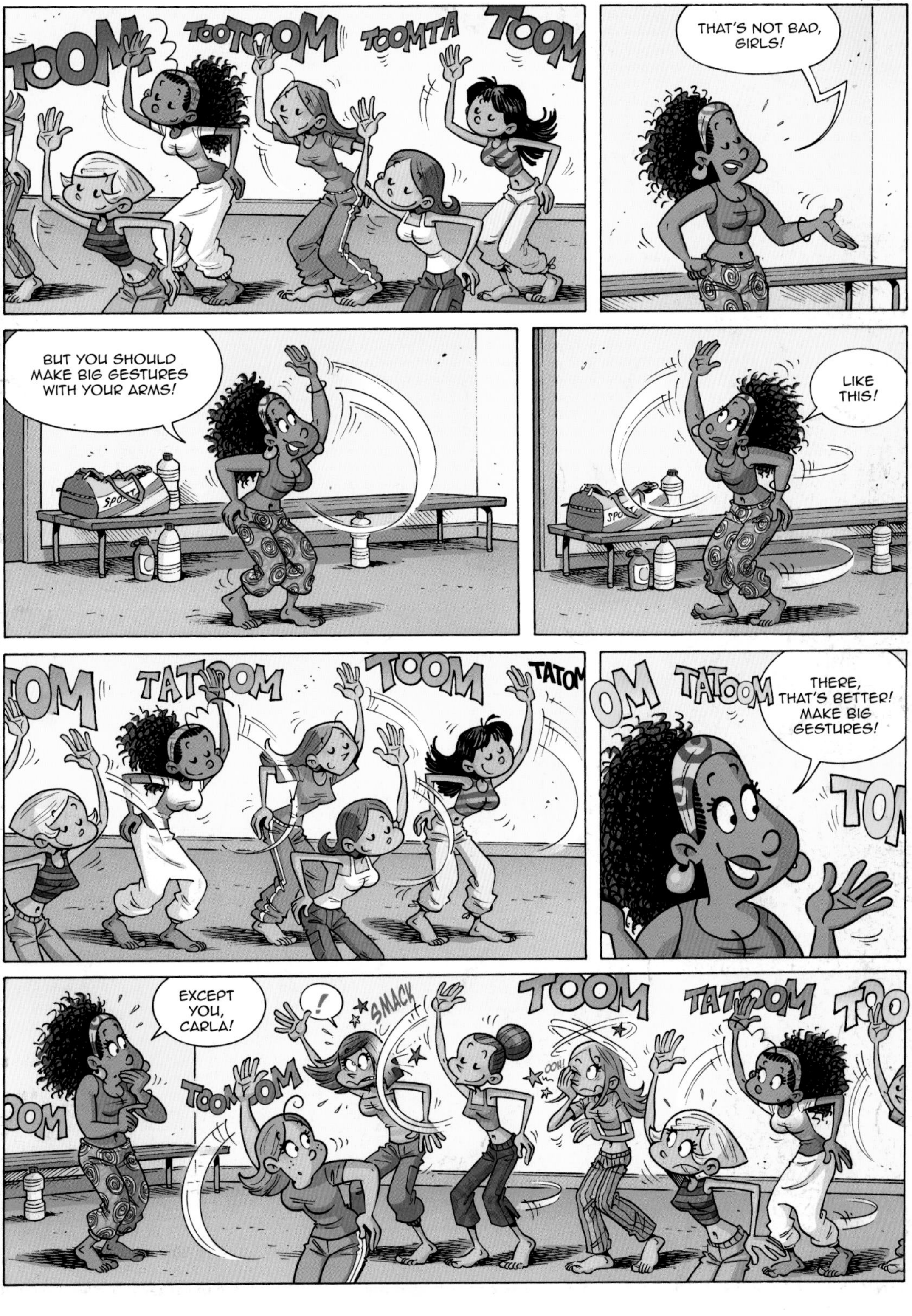
TOOM
TOOTOOM
TOOMTA
TOOM
THAT'S NOT BAD, GIRLS!
BUT YOU SHOULD MAKE BIG GESTURES WITH YOUR ARMS!
LIKE THIS!
TOOM
TATOOM
TOOM
TATOOM
OM
TATOOM
THERE, THAT'S BETTER! MAKE BIG GESTURES!
TOM
EXCEPT YOU, CARLA!
!
SMACK
OOH!
TOOM
TOOM
TATOOM
TOO
OOM

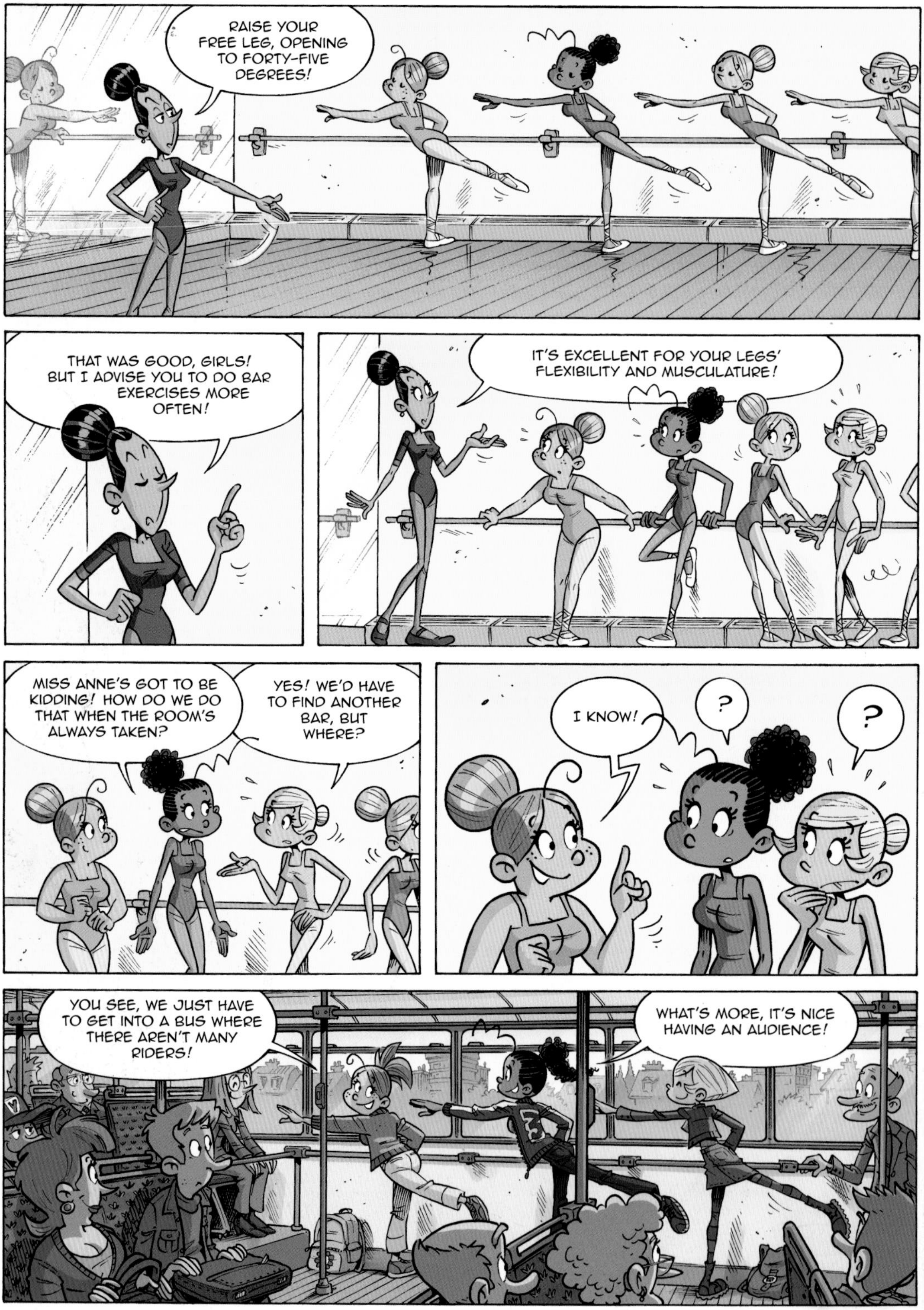
RAISE YOUR FREE LEG, OPENING TO FORTY-FIVE DEGREES!
THAT WAS GOOD, GIRLS! BUT I ADVISE YOU TO DO BAR EXERCISES MORE OFTEN!
IT'S EXCELLENT FOR YOUR LEGS' FLEXIBILITY AND MUSCULATURE!
MISS ANNE'S GOT TO BE KIDDING! HOW DO WE DO THAT WHEN THE ROOM'S ALWAYS TAKEN?
YES! WE'D HAVE TO FIND ANOTHER BAR, BUT WHERE?
I KNOW!
?
?
YOU SEE, WE JUST HAVE TO GET INTO A BUS WHERE THERE AREN'T MANY RIDERS!
WHAT'S MORE, IT'S NICE HAVING AN AUDIENCE!

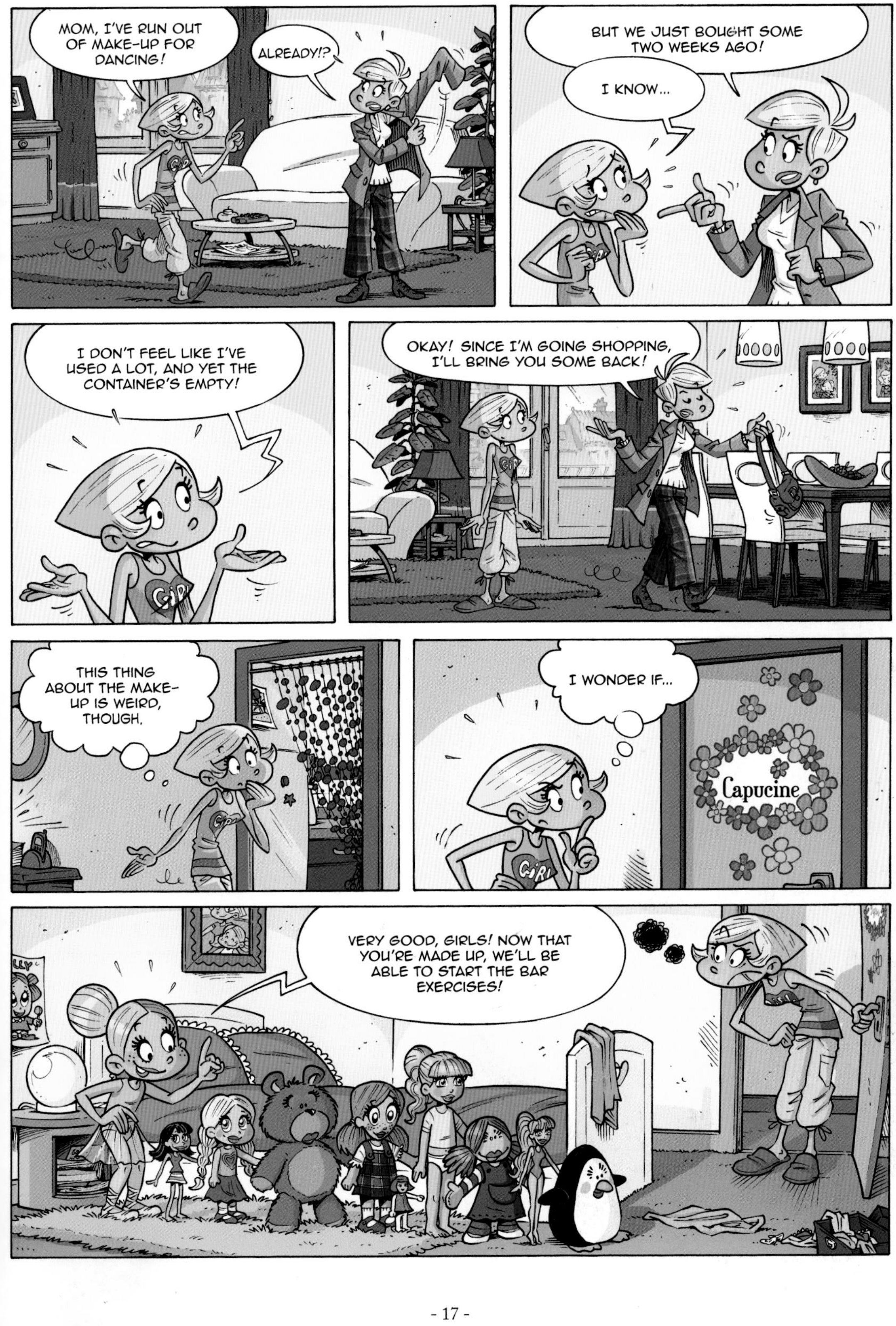
MOM, I'VE RUN OUT OF MAKE-UP FOR DANCING!
ALREADY!?
BUT WE JUST BOUGHT SOME TWO WEEKS AGO!
I KNOW...
I DON'T FEEL LIKE I'VE USED A LOT, AND YET THE CONTAINER'S EMPTY!
OKAY! SINCE I'M GOING SHOPPING, I'LL BRING YOU SOME BACK!
THIS THING ABOUT THE MAKE-UP IS WEIRD, THOUGH.
I WONDER IF...
Capucine
VERY GOOD, GIRLS! NOW THAT YOU'RE MADE UP, WE'LL BE ABLE TO START THE BAR EXERCISES!

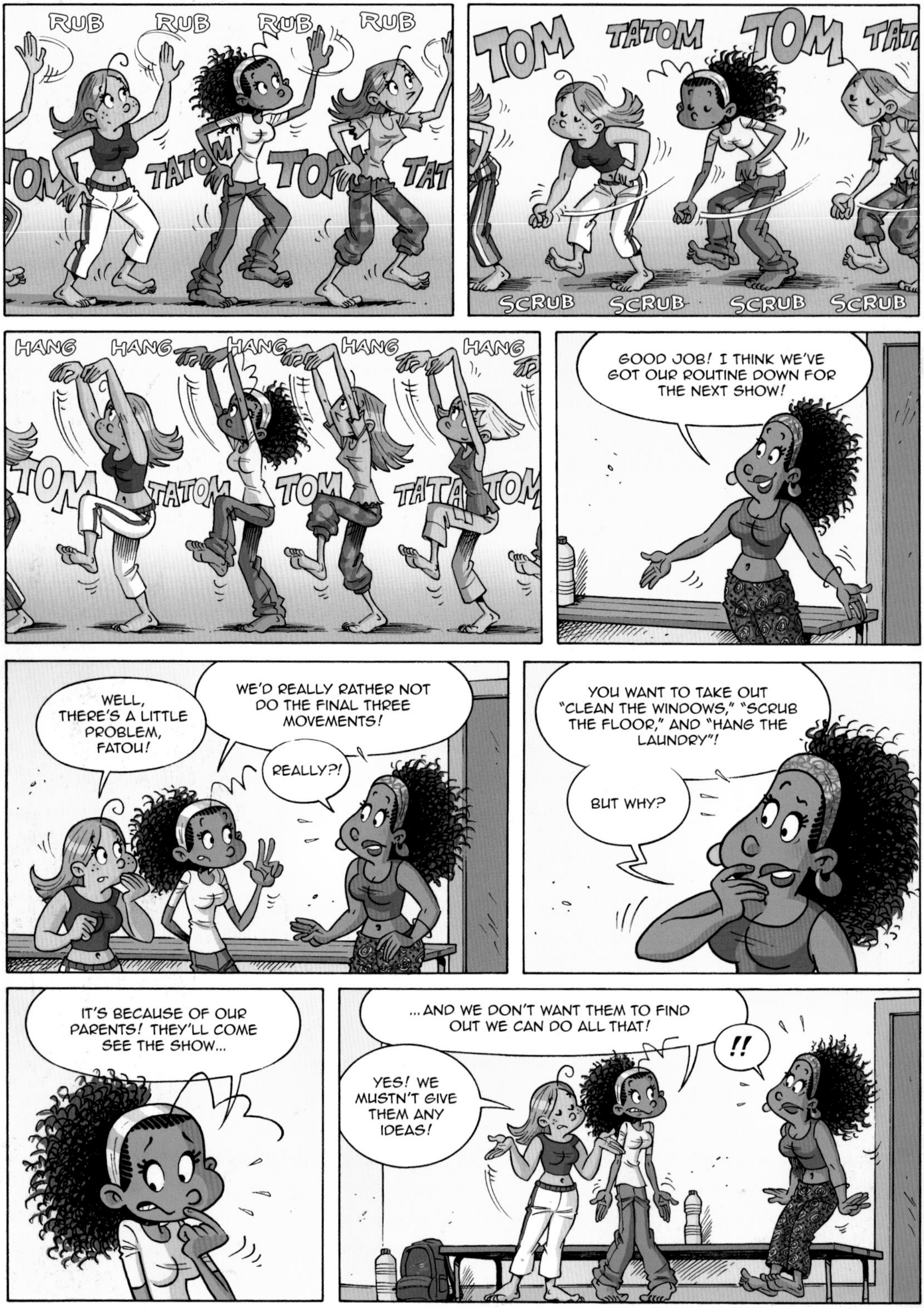
RUB RUB RUB RUB
TOM TATOM TOM TAT
TOM TATOM TOM TAT
SCRUB SCRUB SCRUB SCRUB
HANG HANG HANG HANG HANG
TOM TATOM TOM TATATOM
GOOD JOB! I THINK WE'VE GOT OUR ROUTINE DOWN FOR THE NEXT SHOW!
WELL, THERE'S A LITTLE PROBLEM, FATOU!
WE'D REALLY RATHER NOT DO THE FINAL THREE MOVEMENTS!
REALLY?!
YOU WANT TO TAKE OUT "CLEAN THE WINDOWS," "SCRUB THE FLOOR," AND "HANG THE LAUNDRY"!
BUT WHY?
IT'S BECAUSE OF OUR PARENTS! THEY'LL COME SEE THE SHOW...
...AND WE DON'T WANT THEM TO FIND OUT WE CAN DO ALL THAT!
YES! WE MUSTN'T GIVE THEM ANY IDEAS!
!!

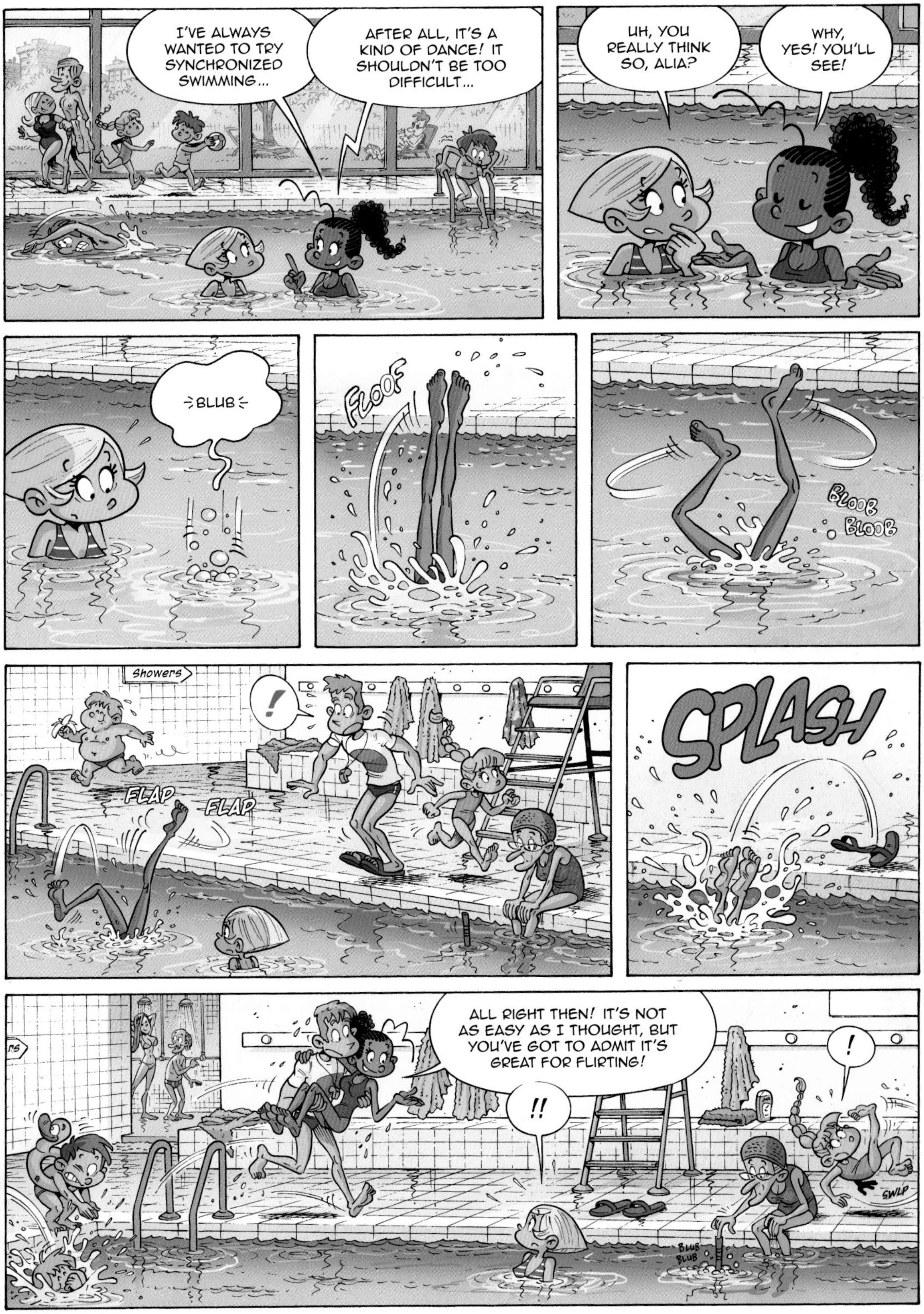
I'VE ALWAYS WANTED TO TRY SYNCHRONIZED SWIMMING...
AFTER ALL, IT'S A KIND OF DANCE! IT SHOULDN'T BE TOO DIFFICULT...
UH, YOU REALLY THINK SO, ALIA?
WHY, YES! YOU'LL SEE!
BLUB
FLOOF
BLOOB
BLOOB
Showers
!
FLAP
FLAP
SPLASH
ALL RIGHT THEN! IT'S NOT AS EASY AS I THOUGHT, BUT YOU'VE GOT TO ADMIT IT'S GREAT FOR FLIRTING!
!!
!
SWLP
BLUB
BLUB

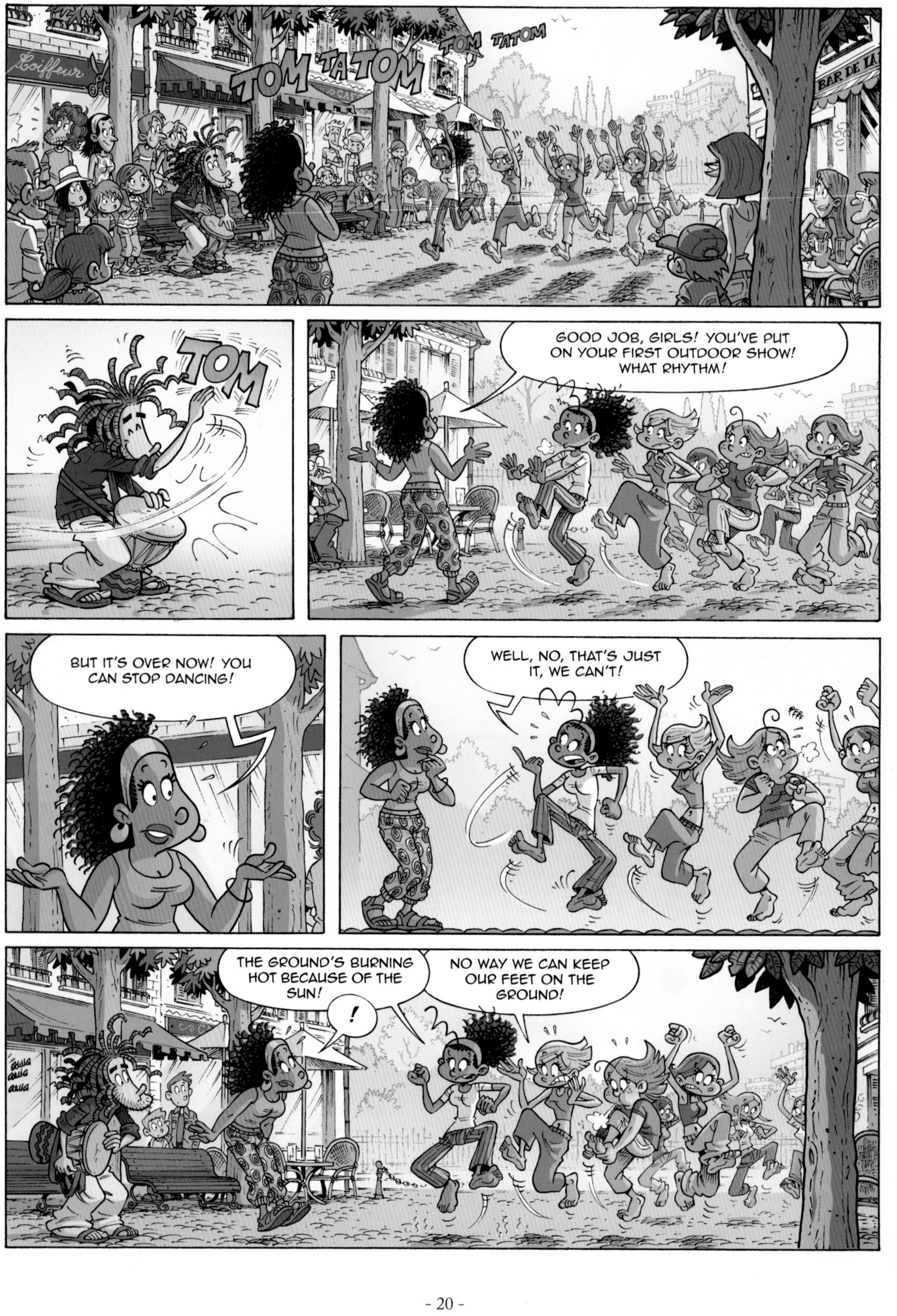
TOM TA TOM
TOM TATOM
TOM
GOOD JOB, GIRLS! YOU'VE PUT ON YOUR FIRST OUTDOOR SHOW! WHAT RHYTHM!
BUT IT'S OVER NOW! YOU CAN STOP DANCING!
WELL, NO, THAT'S JUST IT, WE CAN'T!
THE GROUND'S BURNING HOT BECAUSE OF THE SUN!
!
NO WAY WE CAN KEEP OUR FEET ON THE GROUND!

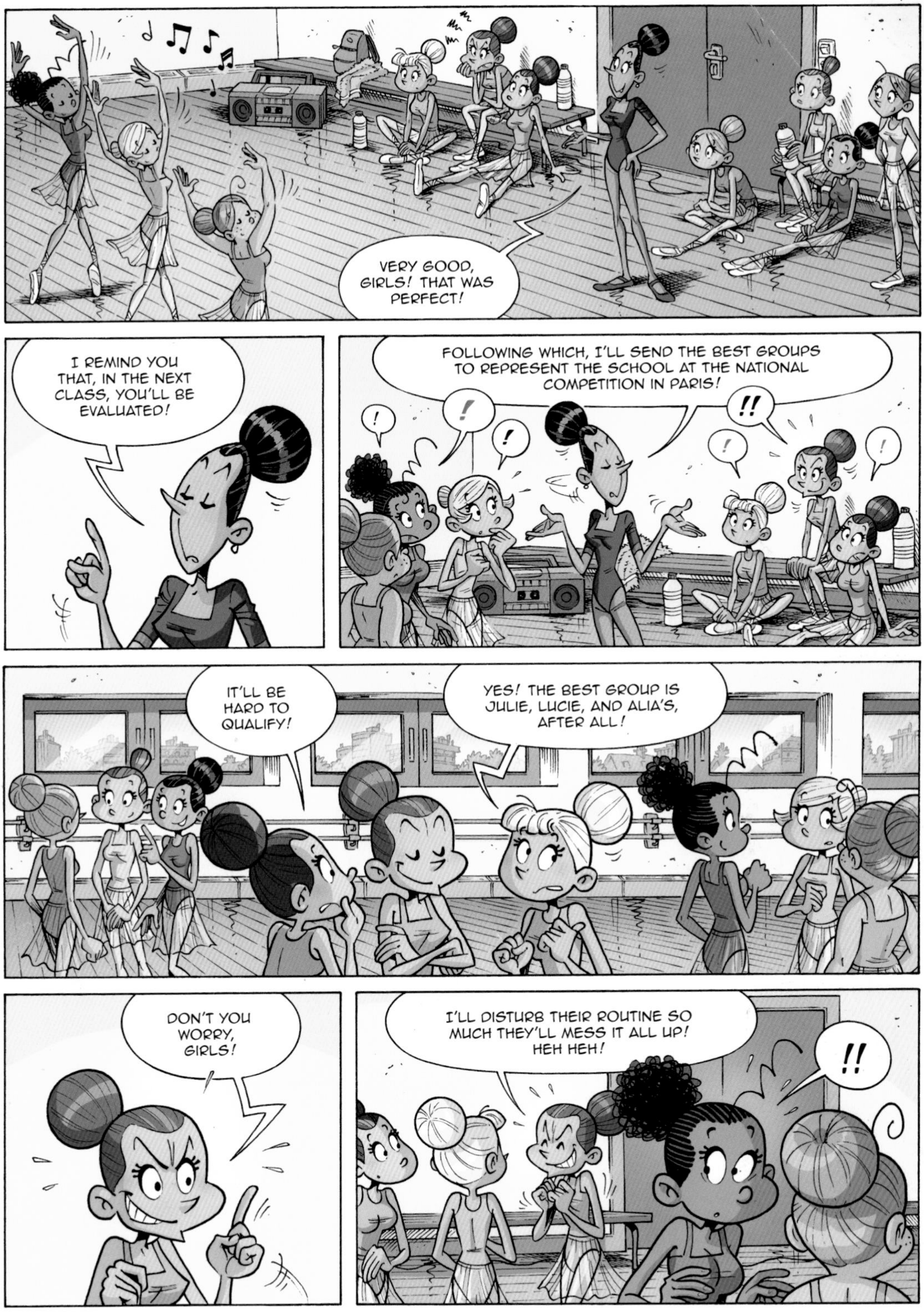
VERY GOOD, GIRLS! THAT WAS PERFECT!
I REMIND YOU THAT, IN THE NEXT CLASS, YOU'LL BE EVALUATED!
FOLLOWING WHICH, I'LL SEND THE BEST GROUPS TO REPRESENT THE SCHOOL AT THE NATIONAL COMPETITION IN PARIS!
!
!
!
!!
!
!
IT'LL BE HARD TO QUALIFY!
YES! THE BEST GROUP IS JULIE, LUCIE, AND ALIA'S, AFTER ALL!
DON'T YOU WORRY, GIRLS!
I'LL DISTURB THEIR ROUTINE SO MUCH THEY'LL MESS IT ALL UP! HEH HEH!
!!

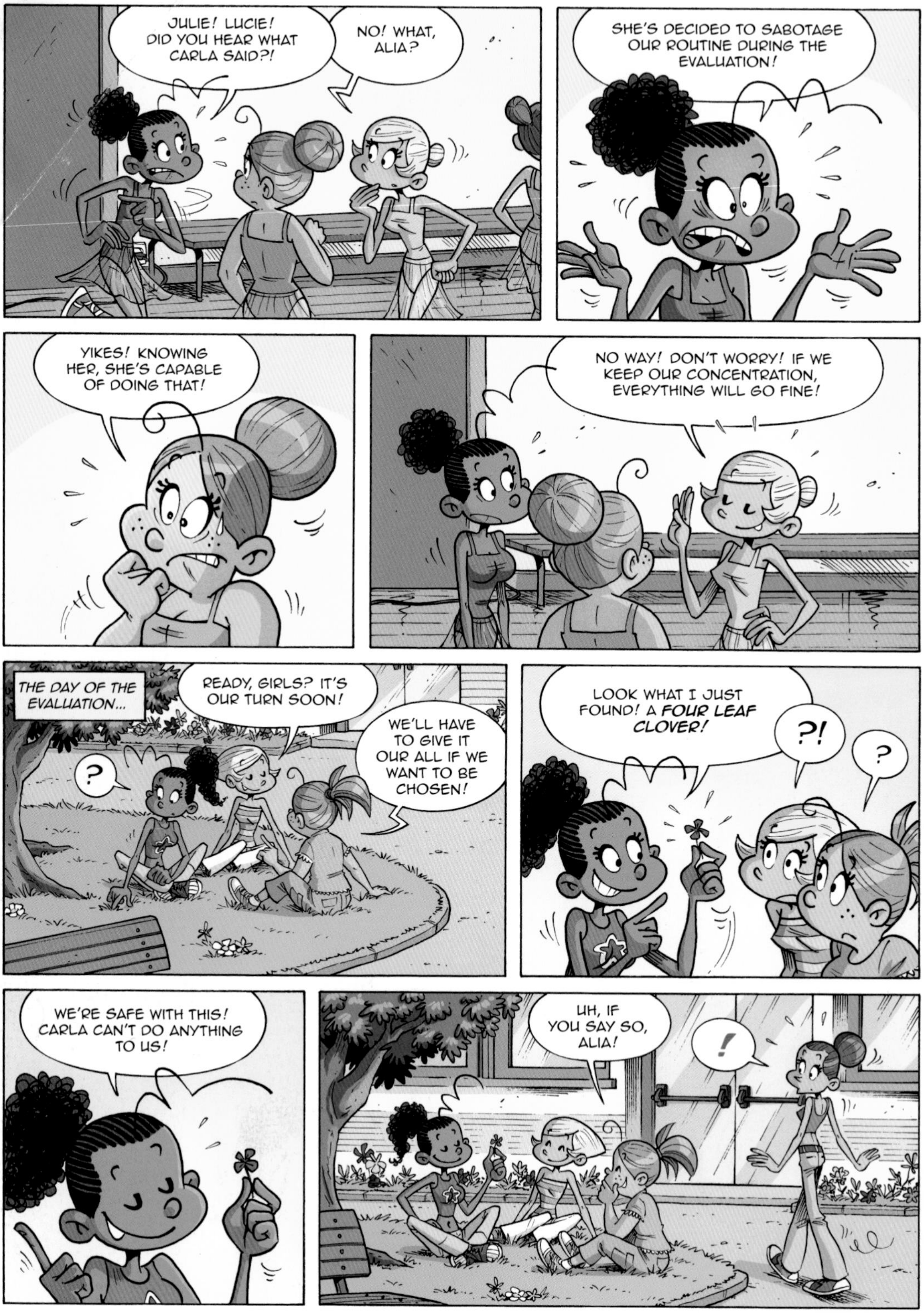
JULIE! LUCIE! DID YOU HEAR WHAT CARLA SAID?!
NO! WHAT, ALIA?
SHE'S DECIDED TO SABOTAGE OUR ROUTINE DURING THE EVALUATION!
YIKES! KNOWING HER, SHE'S CAPABLE OF DOING THAT!
NO WAY! DON'T WORRY! IF WE KEEP OUR CONCENTRATION, EVERYTHING WILL GO FINE!
THE DAY OF THE EVALUATION...
READY, GIRLS? IT'S OUR TURN SOON!
?
WE'LL HAVE TO GIVE IT OUR ALL IF WE WANT TO BE CHOSEN!
LOOK WHAT I JUST FOUND! A **FOUR LEAF CLOVER!**
?!
?
WE'RE SAFE WITH THIS! CARLA CAN'T DO ANYTHING TO US!
UH, IF YOU SAY SO, ALIA!
!

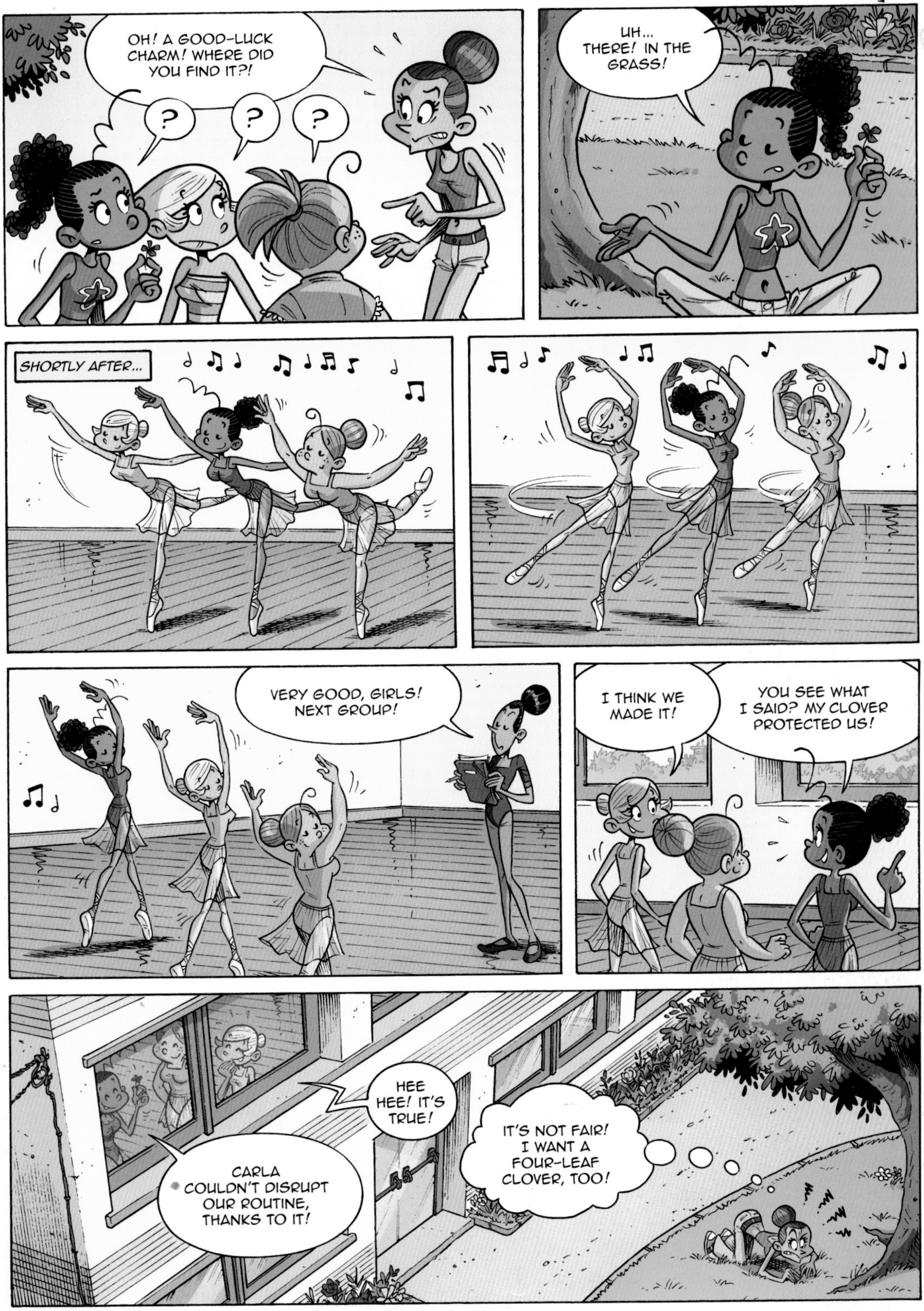
OH! A GOOD-LUCK CHARM! WHERE DID YOU FIND IT?!
?
?
?
UH... THERE! IN THE GRASS!
SHORTLY AFTER...
VERY GOOD, GIRLS! NEXT GROUP!
I THINK WE MADE IT!
YOU SEE WHAT I SAID? MY CLOVER PROTECTED US!
HEE HEE! IT'S TRUE!
CARLA COULDN'T DISRUPT OUR ROUTINE, THANKS TO IT!
IT'S NOT FAIR! I WANT A FOUR-LEAF CLOVER, TOO!

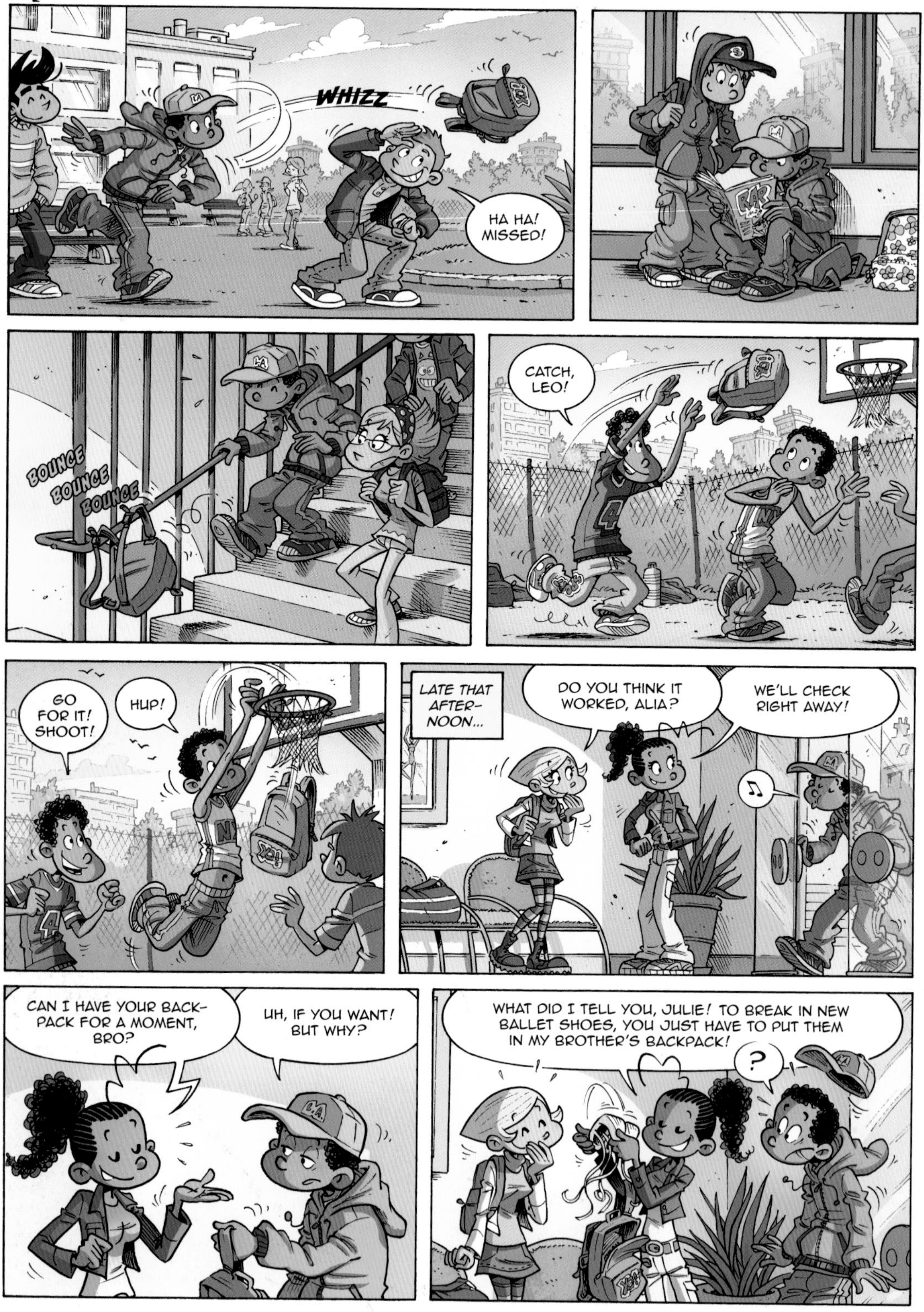
WHIZZ
HA HA! MISSED!
BOUNCE BOUNCE BOUNCE
CATCH, LEO!
GO FOR IT! SHOOT!
HUP!
LATE THAT AFTER-NOON...
DO YOU THINK IT WORKED, ALIA?
WE'LL CHECK RIGHT AWAY!
CAN I HAVE YOUR BACK-PACK FOR A MOMENT, BRO?
UH, IF YOU WANT! BUT WHY?
WHAT DID I TELL YOU, JULIE! TO BREAK IN NEW BALLET SHOES, YOU JUST HAVE TO PUT THEM IN MY BROTHER'S BACKPACK!
?

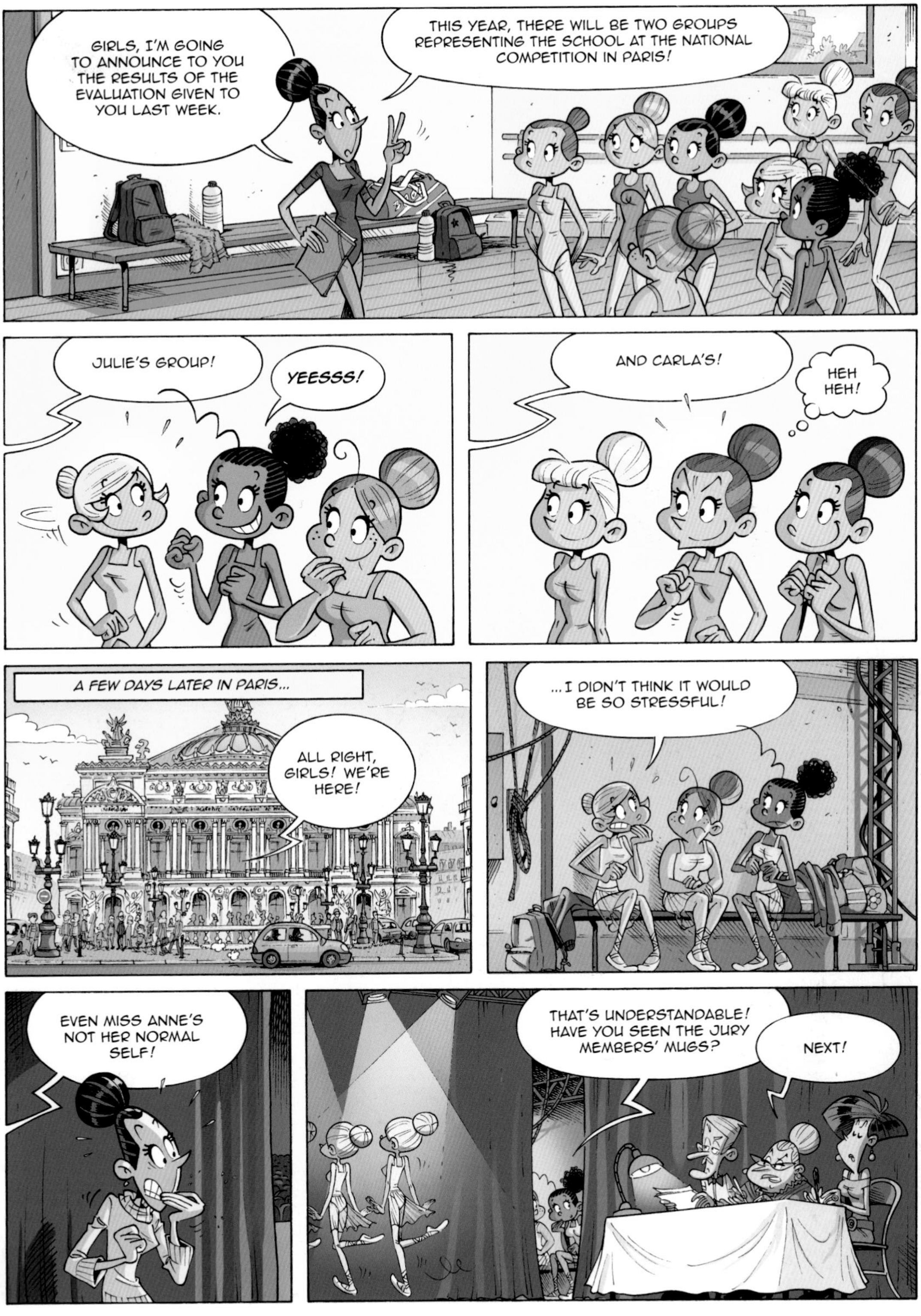
GIRLS, I'M GOING TO ANNOUNCE TO YOU THE RESULTS OF THE EVALUATION GIVEN TO YOU LAST WEEK.
THIS YEAR, THERE WILL BE TWO GROUPS REPRESENTING THE SCHOOL AT THE NATIONAL COMPETITION IN PARIS!
JULIE'S GROUP!
YEESSS!
AND CARLA'S!
HEH HEH!
A FEW DAYS LATER IN PARIS...
ALL RIGHT, GIRLS! WE'RE HERE!
...I DIDN'T THINK IT WOULD BE SO STRESSFUL!
EVEN MISS ANNE'S NOT HER NORMAL SELF!
THAT'S UNDERSTANDABLE! HAVE YOU SEEN THE JURY MEMBERS' MUGS?
NEXT!

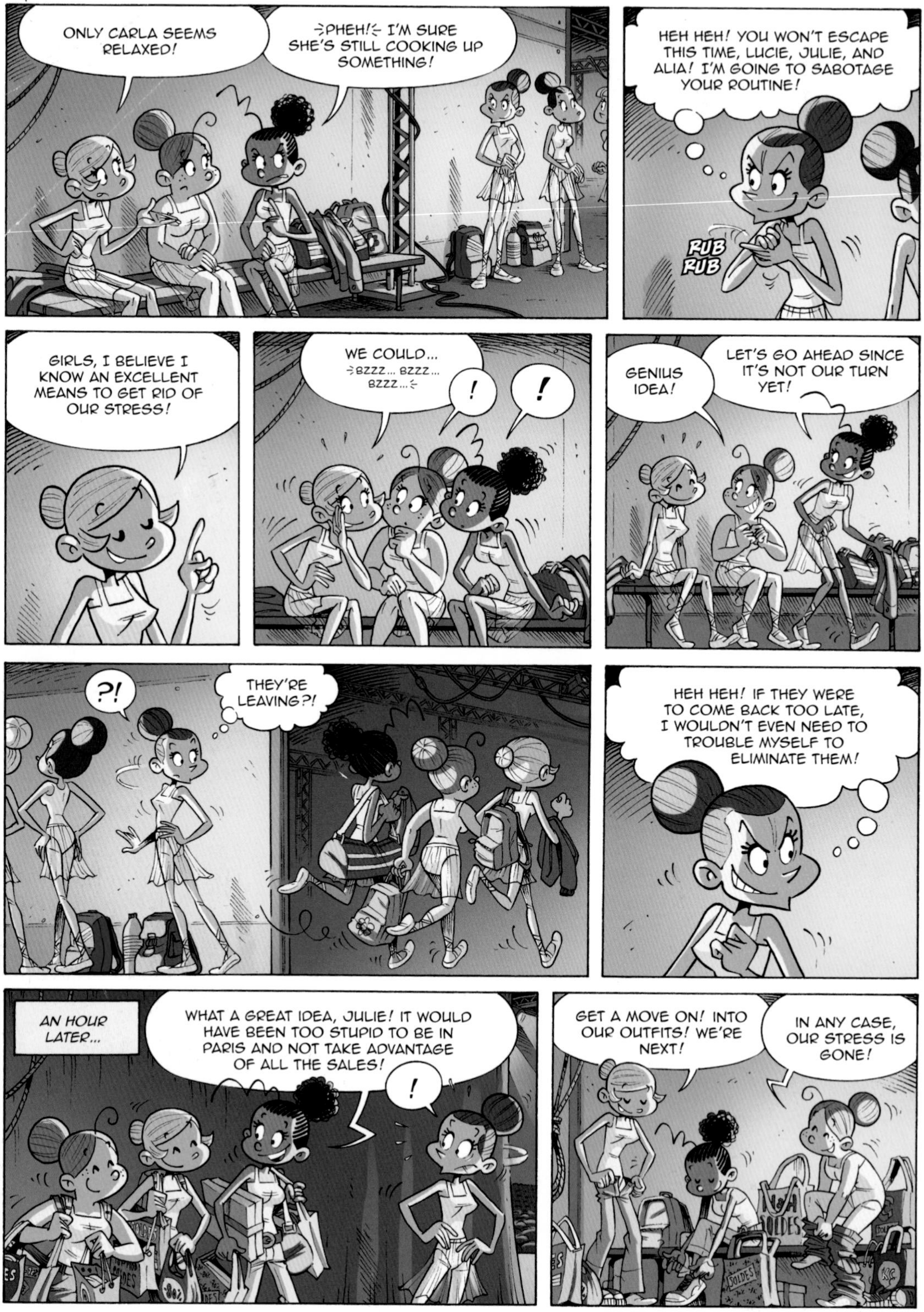
ONLY CARLA SEEMS RELAXED!
PHEH! I'M SURE SHE'S STILL COOKING UP SOMETHING!
HEH HEH! YOU WON'T ESCAPE THIS TIME, LUCIE, JULIE, AND ALIA! I'M GOING TO SABOTAGE YOUR ROUTINE!
RUB RUB
GIRLS, I BELIEVE I KNOW AN EXCELLENT MEANS TO GET RID OF OUR STRESS!
WE COULD... BZZZ... BZZZ... BZZZ...
!
!
GENIUS IDEA!
LET'S GO AHEAD SINCE IT'S NOT OUR TURN YET!
?!
THEY'RE LEAVING?!
HEH HEH! IF THEY WERE TO COME BACK TOO LATE, I WOULDN'T EVEN NEED TO TROUBLE MYSELF TO ELIMINATE THEM!
AN HOUR LATER...
WHAT A GREAT IDEA, JULIE! IT WOULD HAVE BEEN TOO STUPID TO BE IN PARIS AND NOT TAKE ADVANTAGE OF ALL THE SALES!
!
GET A MOVE ON! INTO OUR OUTFITS! WE'RE NEXT!
IN ANY CASE, OUR STRESS IS GONE!

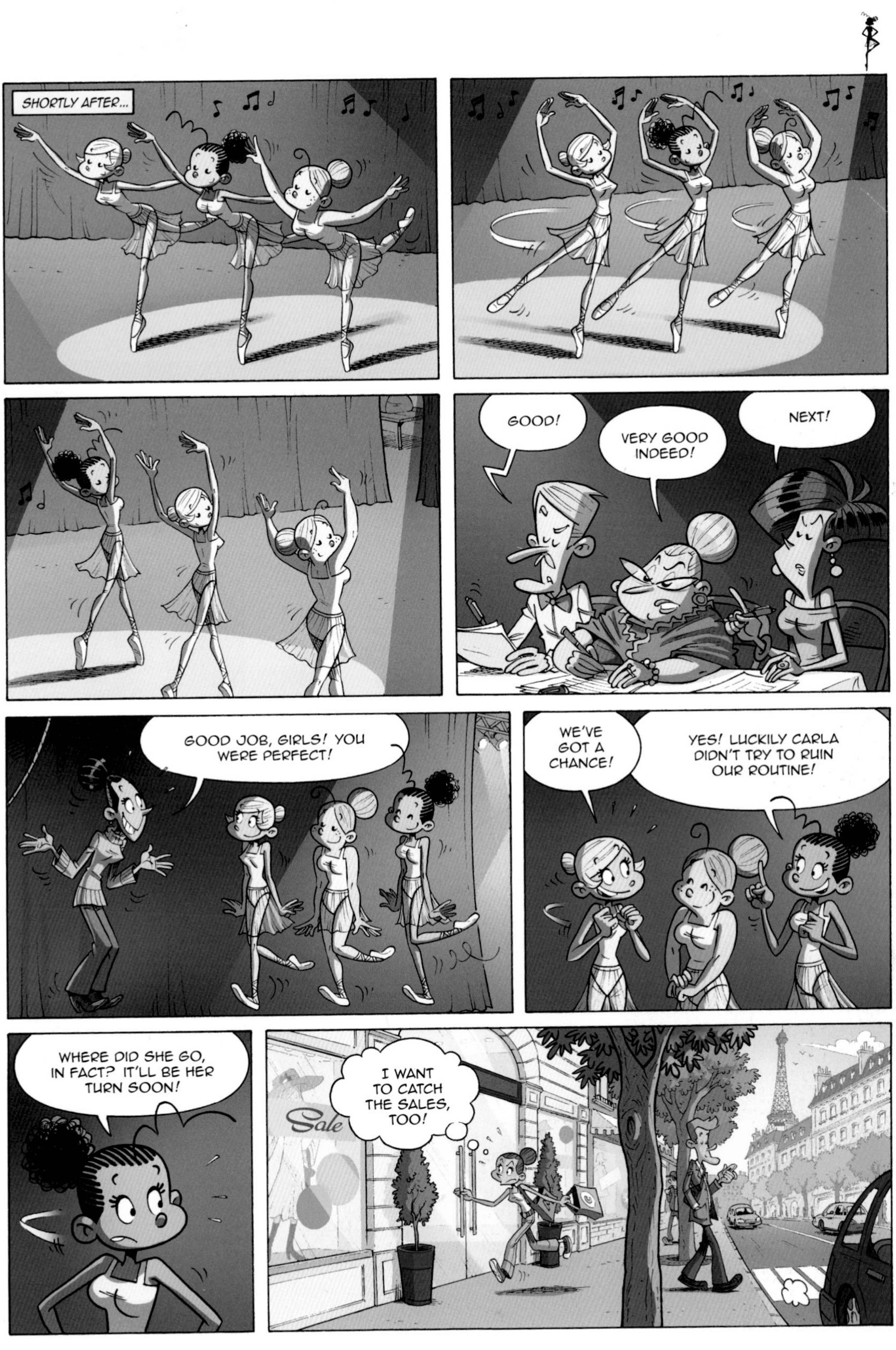
SHORTLY AFTER...
GOOD!
VERY GOOD INDEED!
NEXT!
GOOD JOB, GIRLS! YOU WERE PERFECT!
WE'VE GOT A CHANCE!
YES! LUCKILY CARLA DIDN'T TRY TO RUIN OUR ROUTINE!
WHERE DID SHE GO, IN FACT? IT'LL BE HER TURN SOON!
Sale
I WANT TO CATCH THE SALES, TOO!

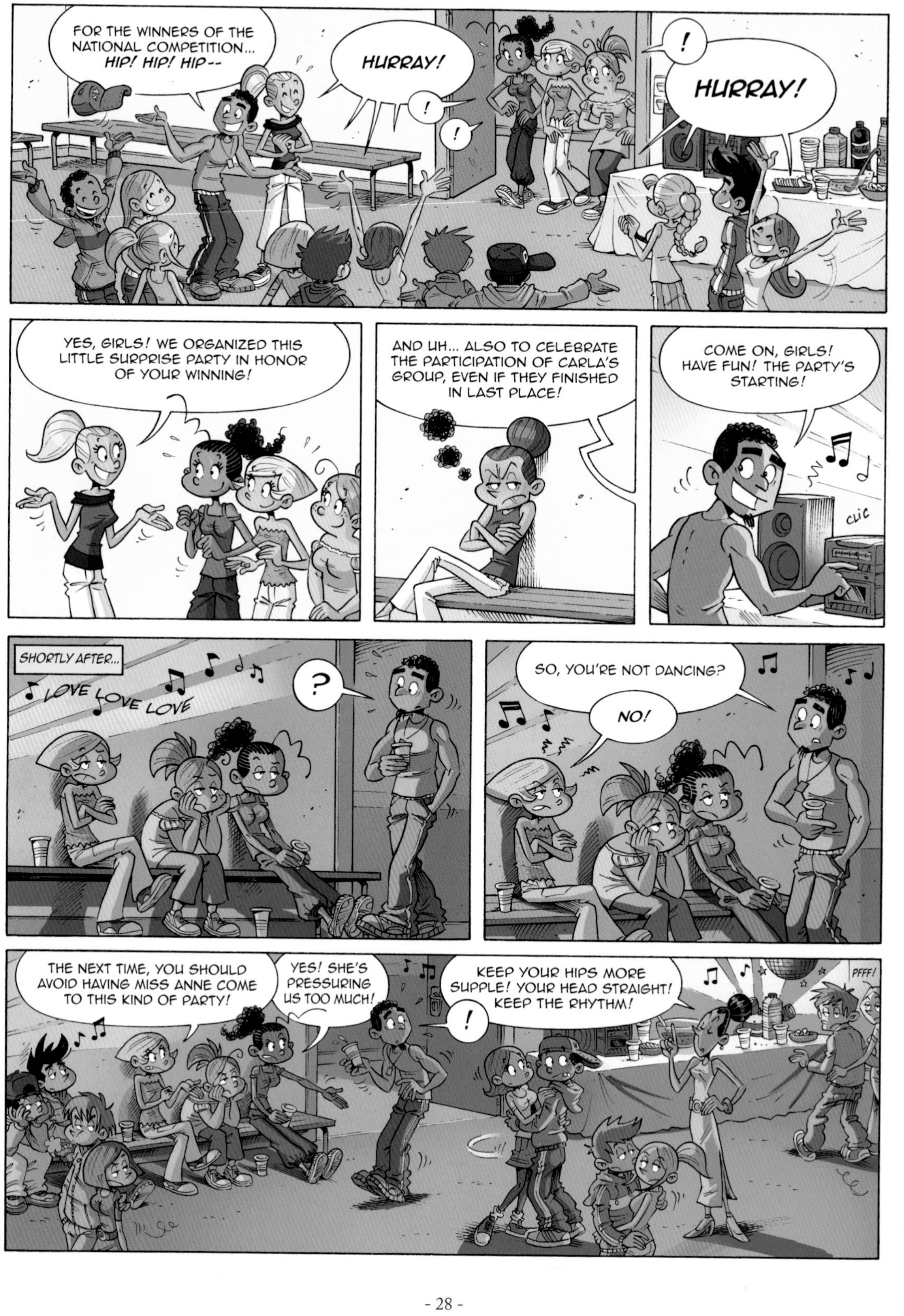
FOR THE WINNERS OF THE NATIONAL COMPETITION... HIP! HIP! HIP--
HURRAY!
!
!
!
HURRAY!
YES, GIRLS! WE ORGANIZED THIS LITTLE SURPRISE PARTY IN HONOR OF YOUR WINNING!
AND UH... ALSO TO CELEBRATE THE PARTICIPATION OF CARLA'S GROUP, EVEN IF THEY FINISHED IN LAST PLACE!
COME ON, GIRLS! HAVE FUN! THE PARTY'S STARTING!
CLIC
SHORTLY AFTER...
LOVE LOVE LOVE
?
SO, YOU'RE NOT DANCING?
NO!
THE NEXT TIME, YOU SHOULD AVOID HAVING MISS ANNE COME TO THIS KIND OF PARTY!
YES! SHE'S PRESSURING US TOO MUCH!
!
KEEP YOUR HIPS MORE SUPPLE! YOUR HEAD STRAIGHT! KEEP THE RHYTHM!
PFFF!

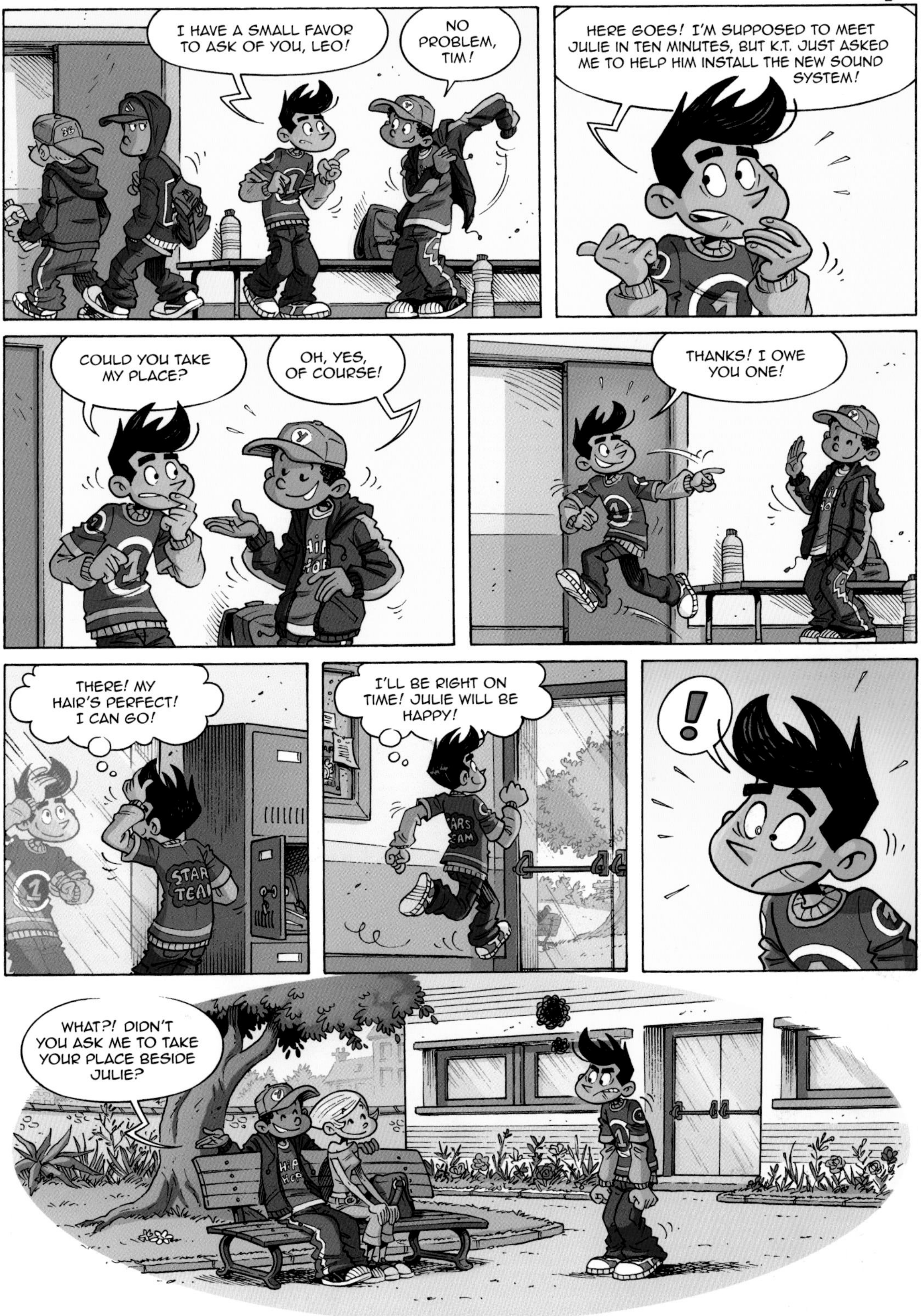
I HAVE A SMALL FAVOR TO ASK OF YOU, LEO!
NO PROBLEM, TIM!
HERE GOES! I'M SUPPOSED TO MEET JULIE IN TEN MINUTES, BUT K.T. JUST ASKED ME TO HELP HIM INSTALL THE NEW SOUND SYSTEM!
COULD YOU TAKE MY PLACE?
OH, YES, OF COURSE!
THANKS! I OWE YOU ONE!
THERE! MY HAIR'S PERFECT! I CAN GO!
I'LL BE RIGHT ON TIME! JULIE WILL BE HAPPY!
!
WHAT?! DIDN'T YOU ASK ME TO TAKE YOUR PLACE BESIDE JULIE?

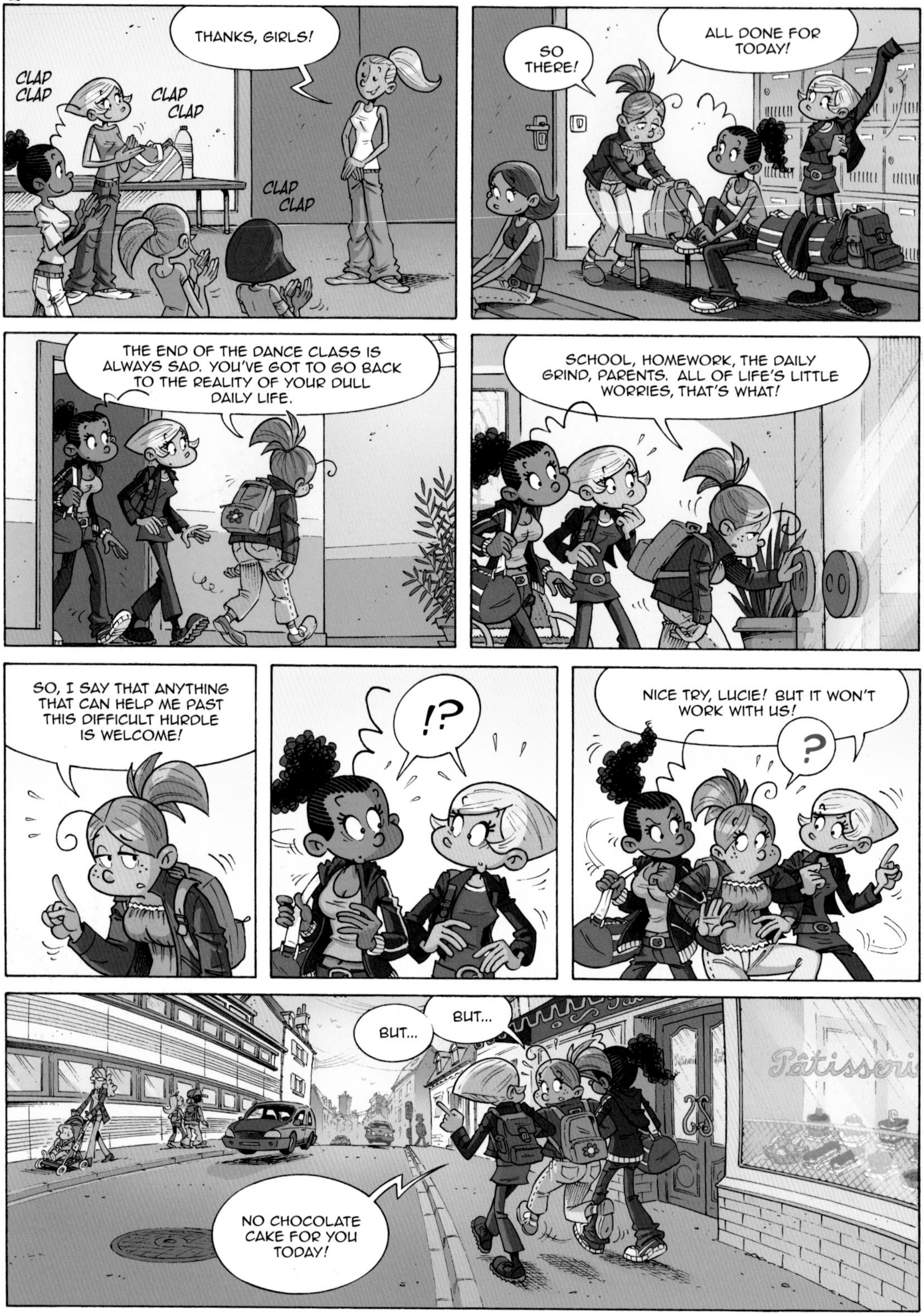
CLAP
CLAP
CLAP
CLAP
THANKS, GIRLS!
CLAP
CLAP
SO THERE!
ALL DONE FOR TODAY!
THE END OF THE DANCE CLASS IS ALWAYS SAD. YOU'VE GOT TO GO BACK TO THE REALITY OF YOUR DULL DAILY LIFE.
SCHOOL, HOMEWORK, THE DAILY GRIND, PARENTS. ALL OF LIFE'S LITTLE WORRIES, THAT'S WHAT!
SO, I SAY THAT ANYTHING THAT CAN HELP ME PAST THIS DIFFICULT HURDLE IS WELCOME!
!?
NICE TRY, LUCIE! BUT IT WON'T WORK WITH US!
?
BUT...
BUT...
Pâtisserie
NO CHOCOLATE CAKE FOR YOU TODAY!

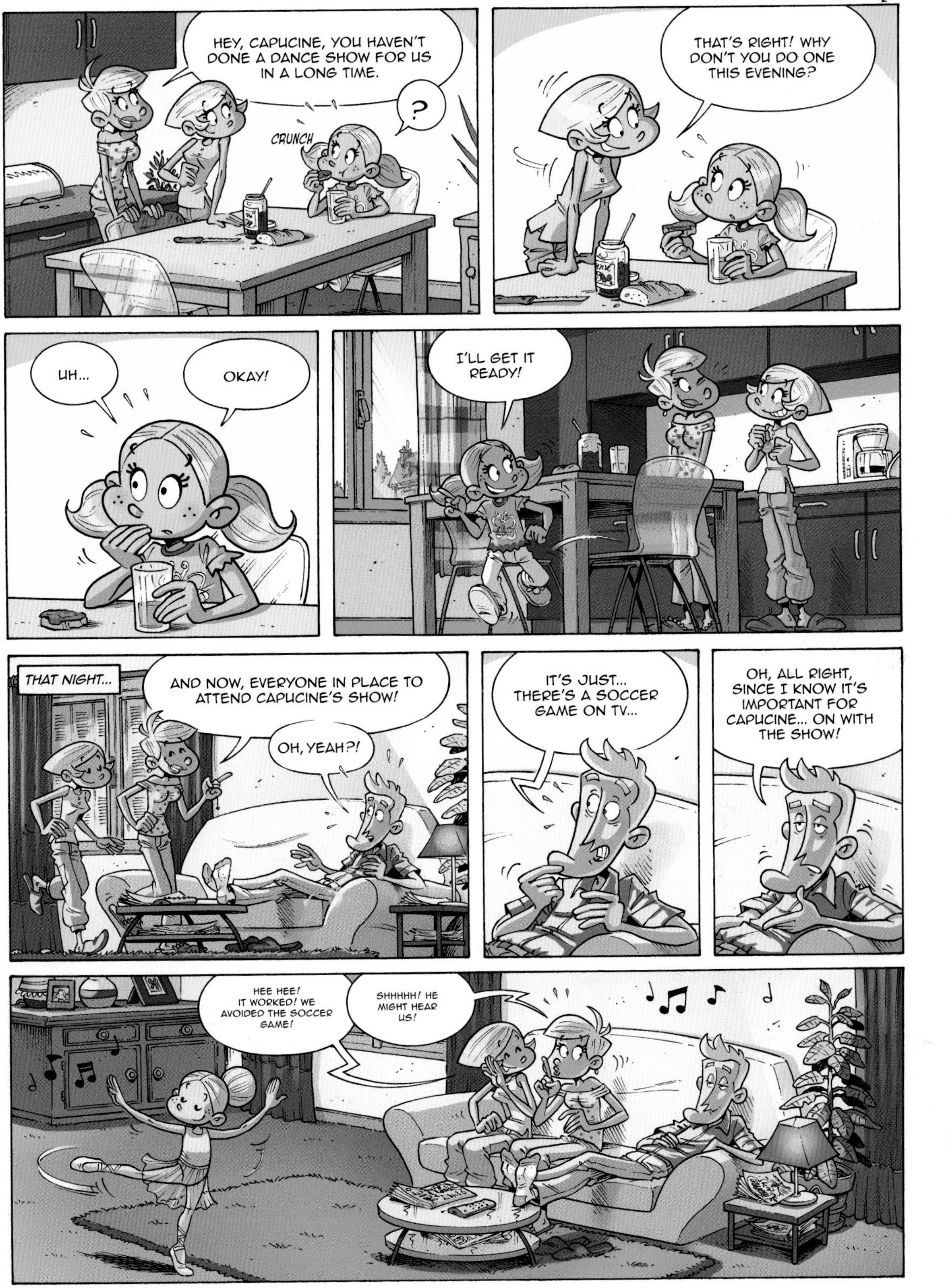
HEY, CAPUCINE, YOU HAVEN'T DONE A DANCE SHOW FOR US IN A LONG TIME.
?
CRUNCH
THAT'S RIGHT! WHY DON'T YOU DO ONE THIS EVENING?
UH...
OKAY!
I'LL GET IT READY!
THAT NIGHT...
AND NOW, EVERYONE IN PLACE TO ATTEND CAPUCINE'S SHOW!
OH, YEAH?!
IT'S JUST... THERE'S A SOCCER GAME ON TV...
OH, ALL RIGHT, SINCE I KNOW IT'S IMPORTANT FOR CAPUCINE... ON WITH THE SHOW!
HEE HEE! IT WORKED! WE AVOIDED THE SOCCER GAME!
SHHHHH! HE MIGHT HEAR US!

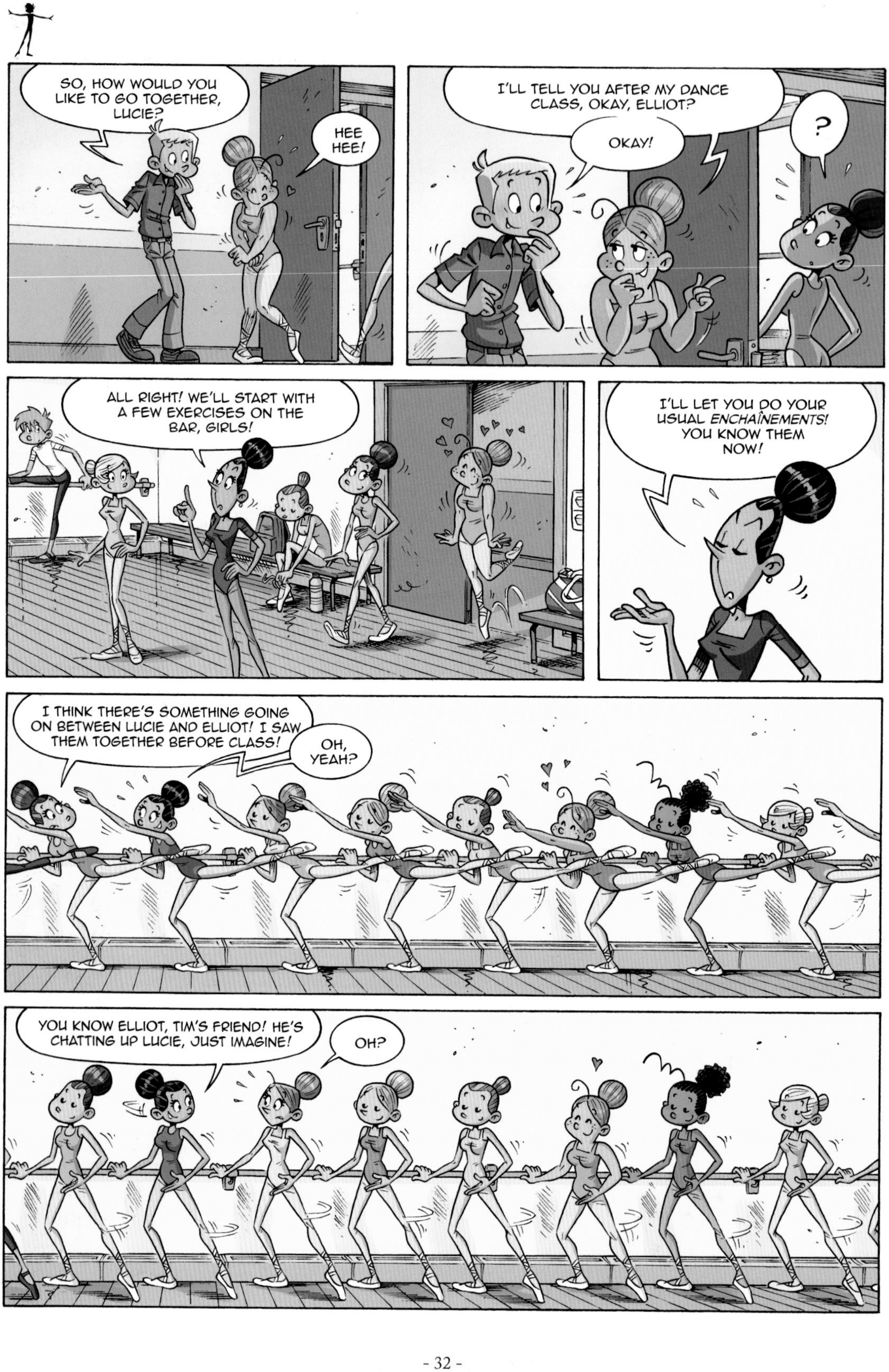

SO, HOW WOULD YOU LIKE TO GO TOGETHER, LUCIE?
HEE HEE!
I'LL TELL YOU AFTER MY DANCE CLASS, OKAY, ELLIOT?
OKAY!
?
ALL RIGHT! WE'LL START WITH A FEW EXERCISES ON THE BAR, GIRLS!
I'LL LET YOU DO YOUR USUAL *ENCHAÎNEMENTS*! YOU KNOW THEM NOW!
I THINK THERE'S SOMETHING GOING ON BETWEEN LUCIE AND ELLIOT! I SAW THEM TOGETHER BEFORE CLASS!
OH, YEAH?
YOU KNOW ELLIOT, TIM'S FRIEND! HE'S CHATTING UP LUCIE, JUST IMAGINE!
OH?

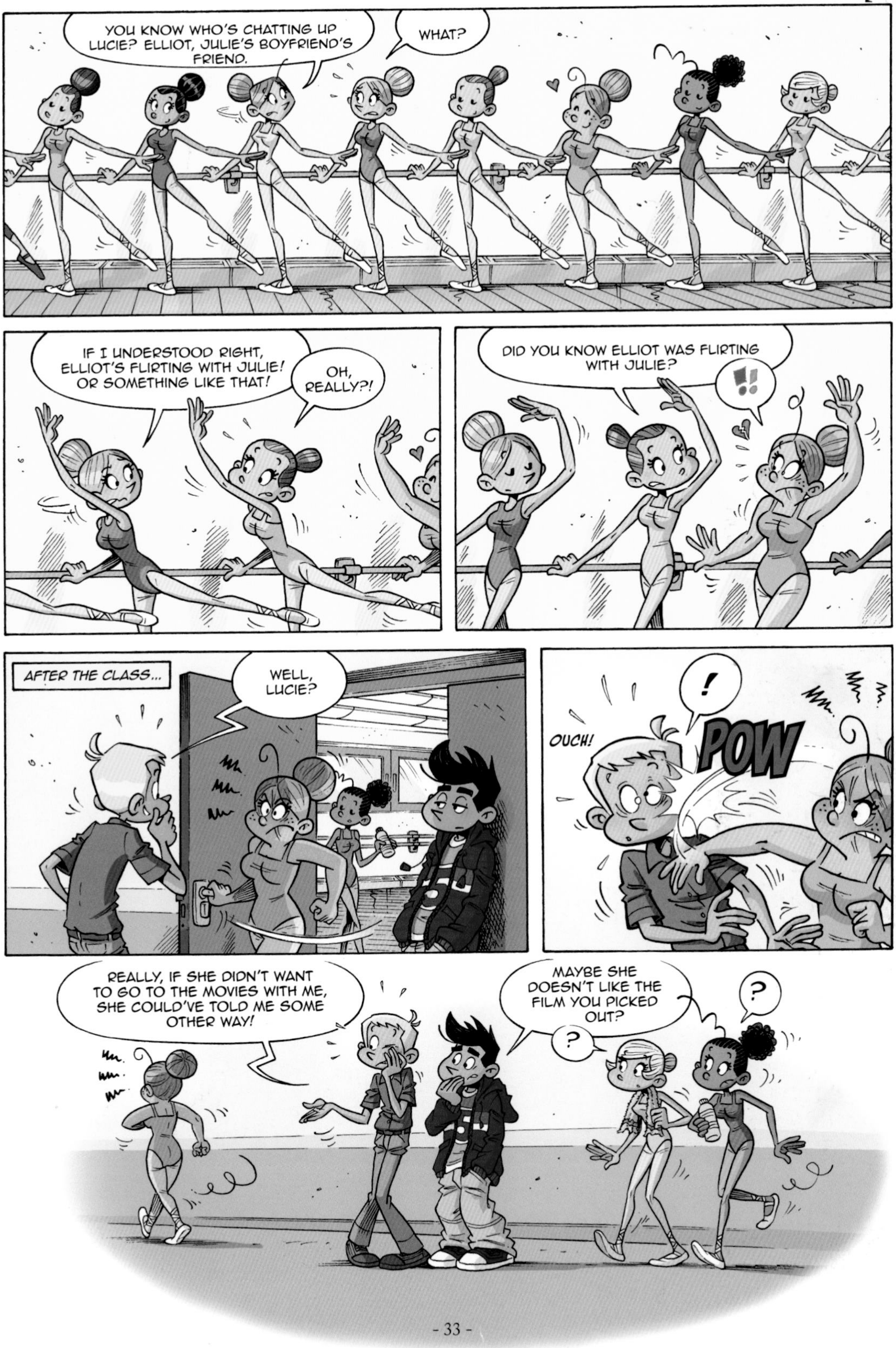
YOU KNOW WHO'S CHATTING UP LUCIE? ELLIOT, JULIE'S BOYFRIEND'S FRIEND.
WHAT?
IF I UNDERSTOOD RIGHT, ELLIOT'S FLIRTING WITH JULIE! OR SOMETHING LIKE THAT!
OH, REALLY?!
DID YOU KNOW ELLIOT WAS FLIRTING WITH JULIE?
!!
AFTER THE CLASS...
WELL, LUCIE?
OUCH!
!
POW
REALLY, IF SHE DIDN'T WANT TO GO TO THE MOVIES WITH ME, SHE COULD'VE TOLD ME SOME OTHER WAY!
MAYBE SHE DOESN'T LIKE THE FILM YOU PICKED OUT?
?
?

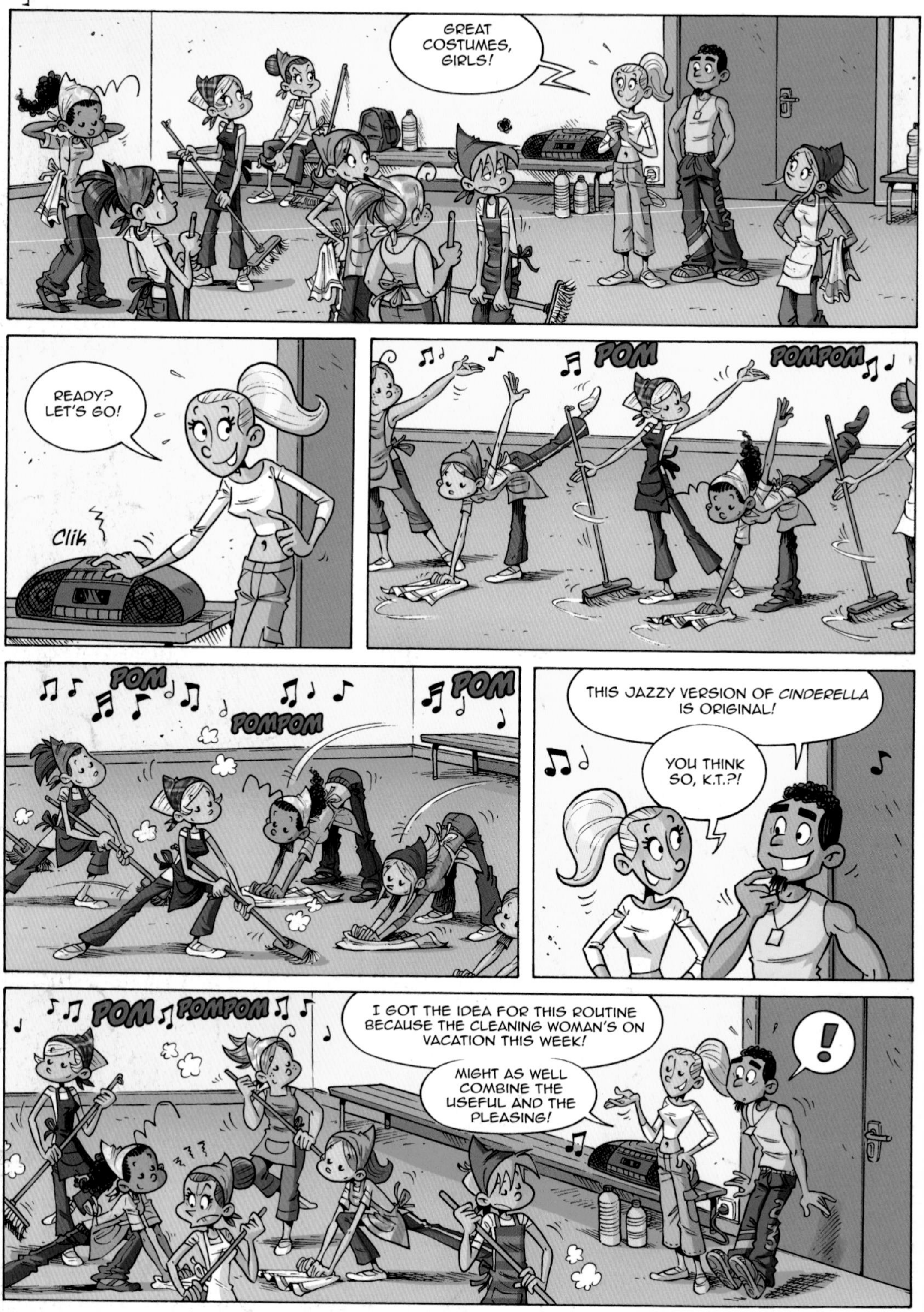
GREAT COSTUMES, GIRLS!
READY? LET'S GO!
Clik
POM
POMPOM
POM
POMPOM
POM
THIS JAZZY VERSION OF *CINDERELLA* IS ORIGINAL!
YOU THINK SO, K.T.?!
POM
POMPOM
I GOT THE IDEA FOR THIS ROUTINE BECAUSE THE CLEANING WOMAN'S ON VACATION THIS WEEK!
MIGHT AS WELL COMBINE THE USEFUL AND THE PLEASING!
!

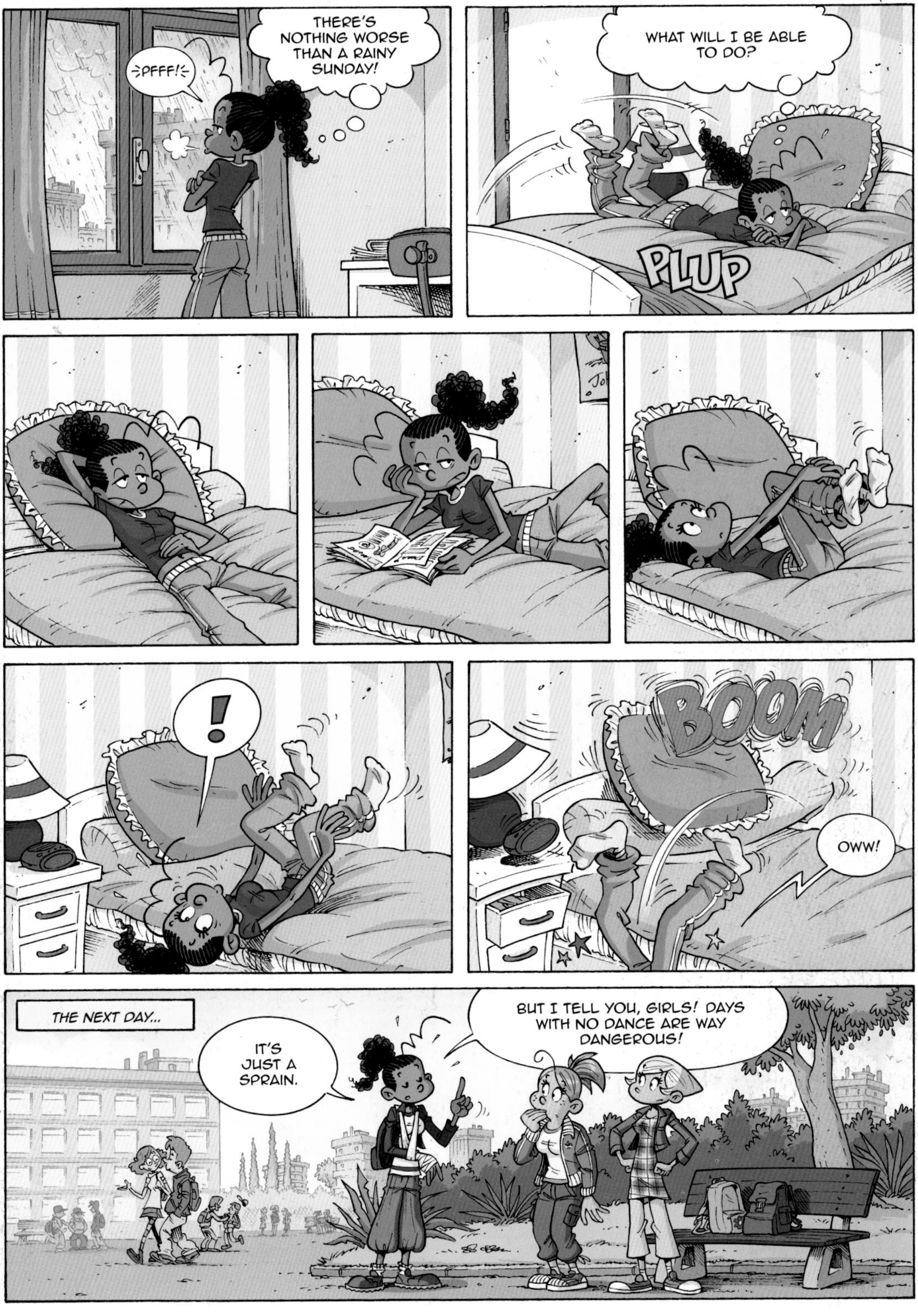
PFFF!
THERE'S NOTHING WORSE THAN A RAINY SUNDAY!
WHAT WILL I BE ABLE TO DO?
PLUP
!
BOOM
OWW!
THE NEXT DAY...
IT'S JUST A SPRAIN.
BUT I TELL YOU, GIRLS! DAYS WITH NO DANCE ARE WAY DANGEROUS!

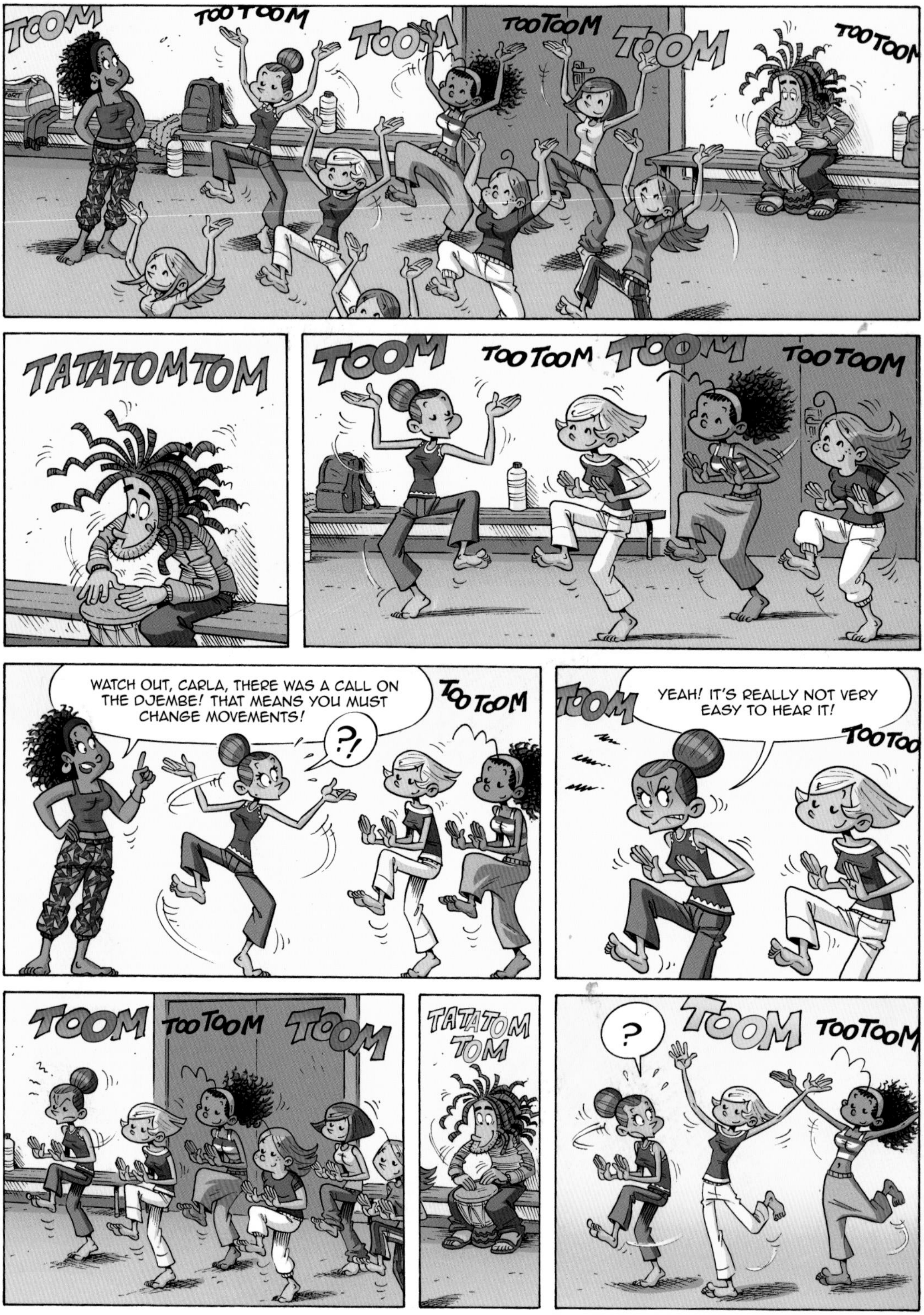
TOOM
TOOTOOM
TOOM
TOOTOOM
TOOM
TOOTOOM
TATATOMTOM
TOOM
TOOTOOM
TOOM
TOOTOOM
WATCH OUT, CARLA, THERE WAS A CALL ON THE DJEMBE! THAT MEANS YOU MUST CHANGE MOVEMENTS!
TOOTOOM
?!
TOOM
YEAH! IT'S REALLY NOT VERY EASY TO HEAR IT!
TOOTOO
TOOM
TOOTOOM
TOOM
TATATOM TOM
?
TOOM
TOOTOOM

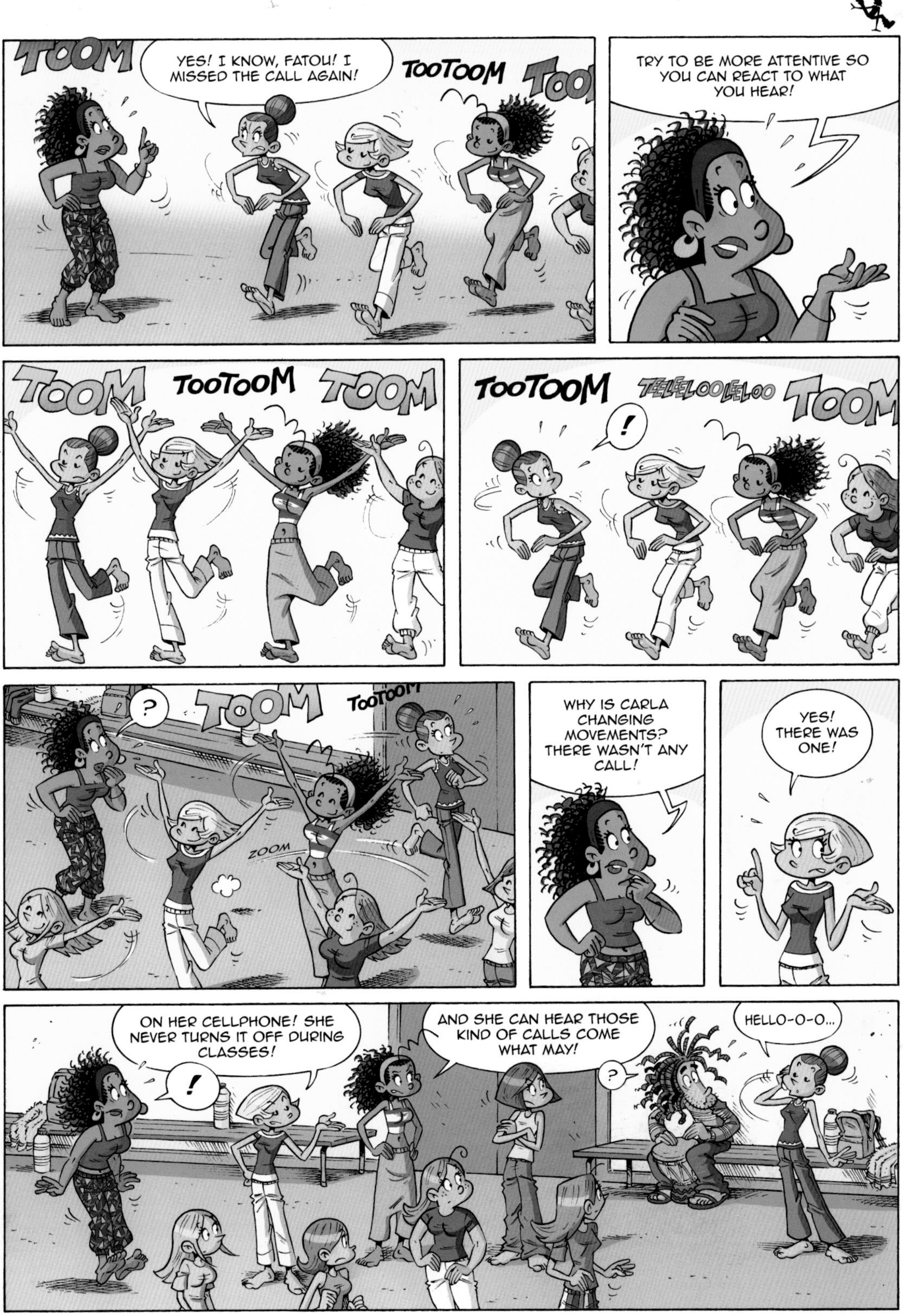
TOOM
YES! I KNOW, FATOU! I MISSED THE CALL AGAIN!
TOOTOOM
TRY TO BE MORE ATTENTIVE SO YOU CAN REACT TO WHAT YOU HEAR!
TOOM
TOOTOOM
TOOM
TOOTOOM
TEELEELOOLEELOO
TOOM
!
?
TOOM
TOOTOOM
ZOOM
WHY IS CARLA CHANGING MOVEMENTS? THERE WASN'T ANY CALL!
YES! THERE WAS ONE!
ON HER CELLPHONE! SHE NEVER TURNS IT OFF DURING CLASSES!
!
AND SHE CAN HEAR THOSE KIND OF CALLS COME WHAT MAY!
?
HELLO-O-O...

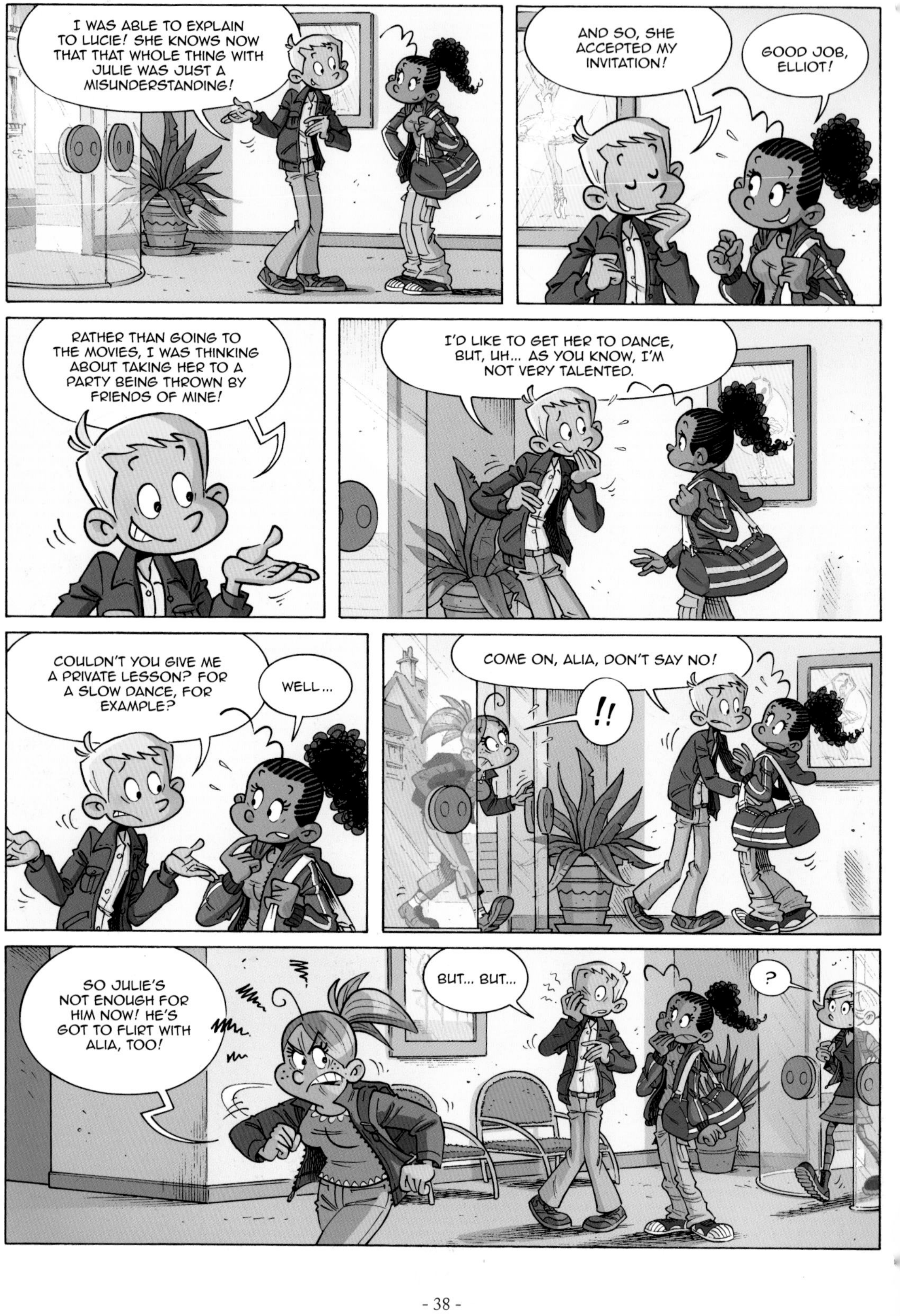
I WAS ABLE TO EXPLAIN TO LUCIE! SHE KNOWS NOW THAT THAT WHOLE THING WITH JULIE WAS JUST A MISUNDERSTANDING!
AND SO, SHE ACCEPTED MY INVITATION!
GOOD JOB, ELLIOT!
RATHER THAN GOING TO THE MOVIES, I WAS THINKING ABOUT TAKING HER TO A PARTY BEING THROWN BY FRIENDS OF MINE!
I'D LIKE TO GET HER TO DANCE, BUT, UH... AS YOU KNOW, I'M NOT VERY TALENTED.
COULDN'T YOU GIVE ME A PRIVATE LESSON? FOR A SLOW DANCE, FOR EXAMPLE?
WELL...
COME ON, ALIA, DON'T SAY NO!
!!
SO JULIE'S NOT ENOUGH FOR HIM NOW! HE'S GOT TO FLIRT WITH ALIA, TOO!
BUT... BUT...
?

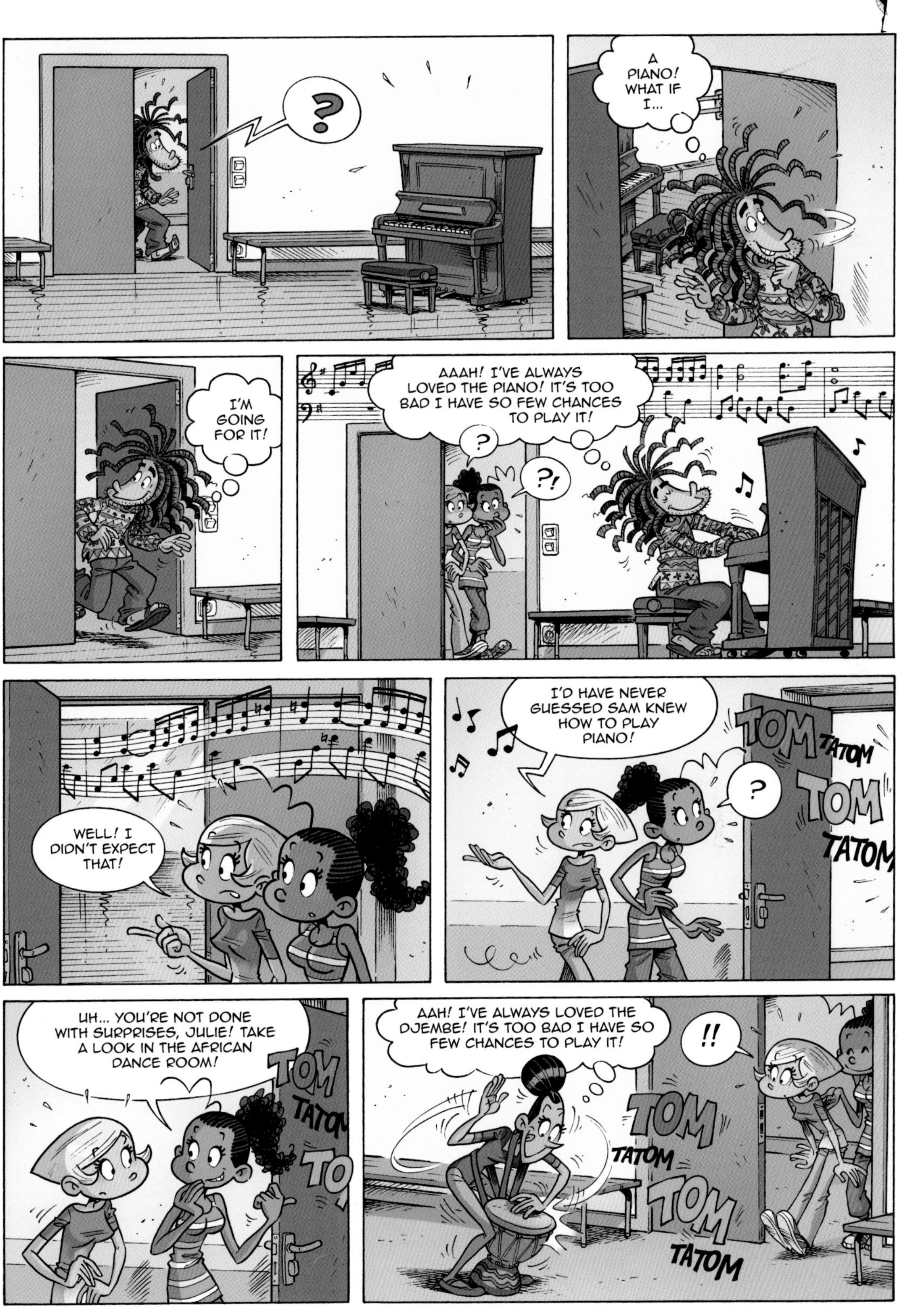
?
A PIANO! WHAT IF I...
I'M GOING FOR IT!
AAAH! I'VE ALWAYS LOVED THE PIANO! IT'S TOO BAD I HAVE SO FEW CHANCES TO PLAY IT!
?
?!
WELL! I DIDN'T EXPECT THAT!
I'D HAVE NEVER GUESSED SAM KNEW HOW TO PLAY PIANO!
?
TOM TATOM TOM TATOM
UH... YOU'RE NOT DONE WITH SURPRISES, JULIE! TAKE A LOOK IN THE AFRICAN DANCE ROOM!
TOM TATOM
AAH! I'VE ALWAYS LOVED THE DJEMBE! IT'S TOO BAD I HAVE SO FEW CHANCES TO PLAY IT!
!!
TOM TATOM TOM TATOM

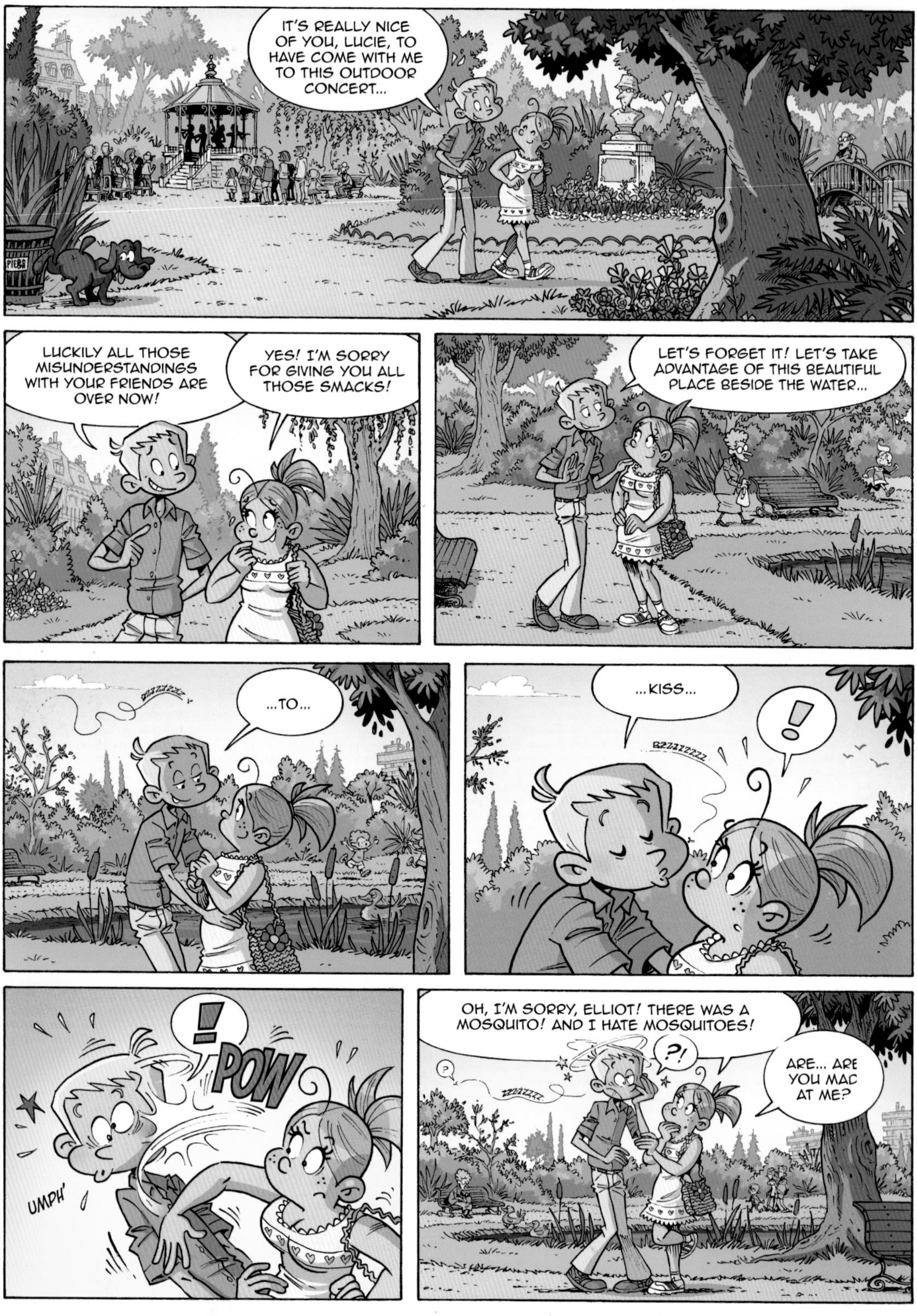
IT'S REALLY NICE OF YOU, LUCIE, TO HAVE COME WITH ME TO THIS OUTDOOR CONCERT...
LUCKILY ALL THOSE MISUNDERSTANDINGS WITH YOUR FRIENDS ARE OVER NOW!
YES! I'M SORRY FOR GIVING YOU ALL THOSE SMACKS!
LET'S FORGET IT! LET'S TAKE ADVANTAGE OF THIS BEAUTIFUL PLACE BESIDE THE WATER...
...TO...
...KISS...
!
!
POW
UMPH'
OH, I'M SORRY, ELLIOT! THERE WAS A MOSQUITO! AND I HATE MOSQUITOES!
?!
ARE... ARE YOU MAD AT ME?

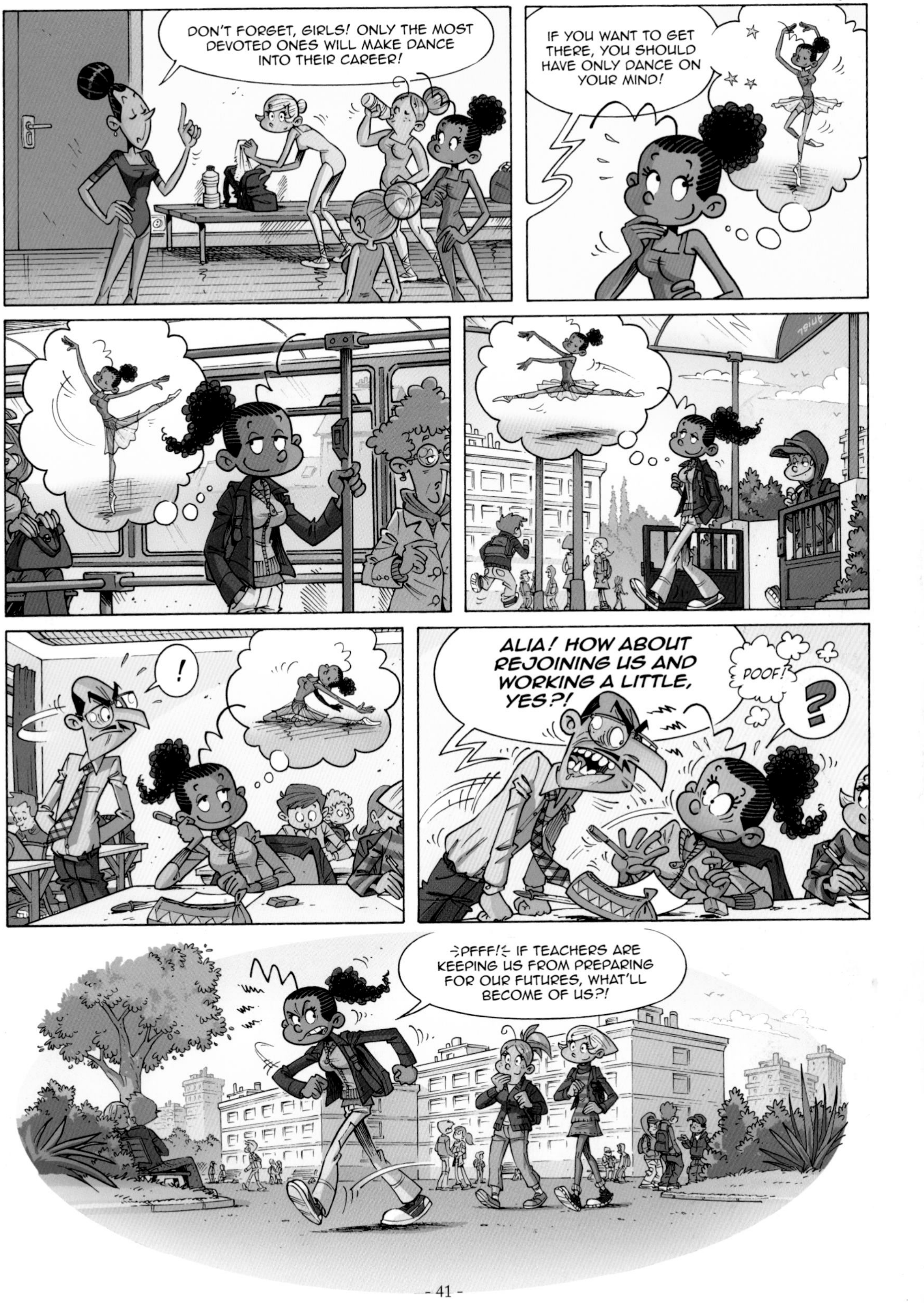

DON'T FORGET, GIRLS! ONLY THE MOST DEVOTED ONES WILL MAKE DANCE INTO THEIR CAREER!
IF YOU WANT TO GET THERE, YOU SHOULD HAVE ONLY DANCE ON YOUR MIND!
!
ALIA! HOW ABOUT REJOINING US AND WORKING A LITTLE, YES?!
POOF!
?
PFFF! IF TEACHERS ARE KEEPING US FROM PREPARING FOR OUR FUTURES, WHAT'LL BECOME OF US?!

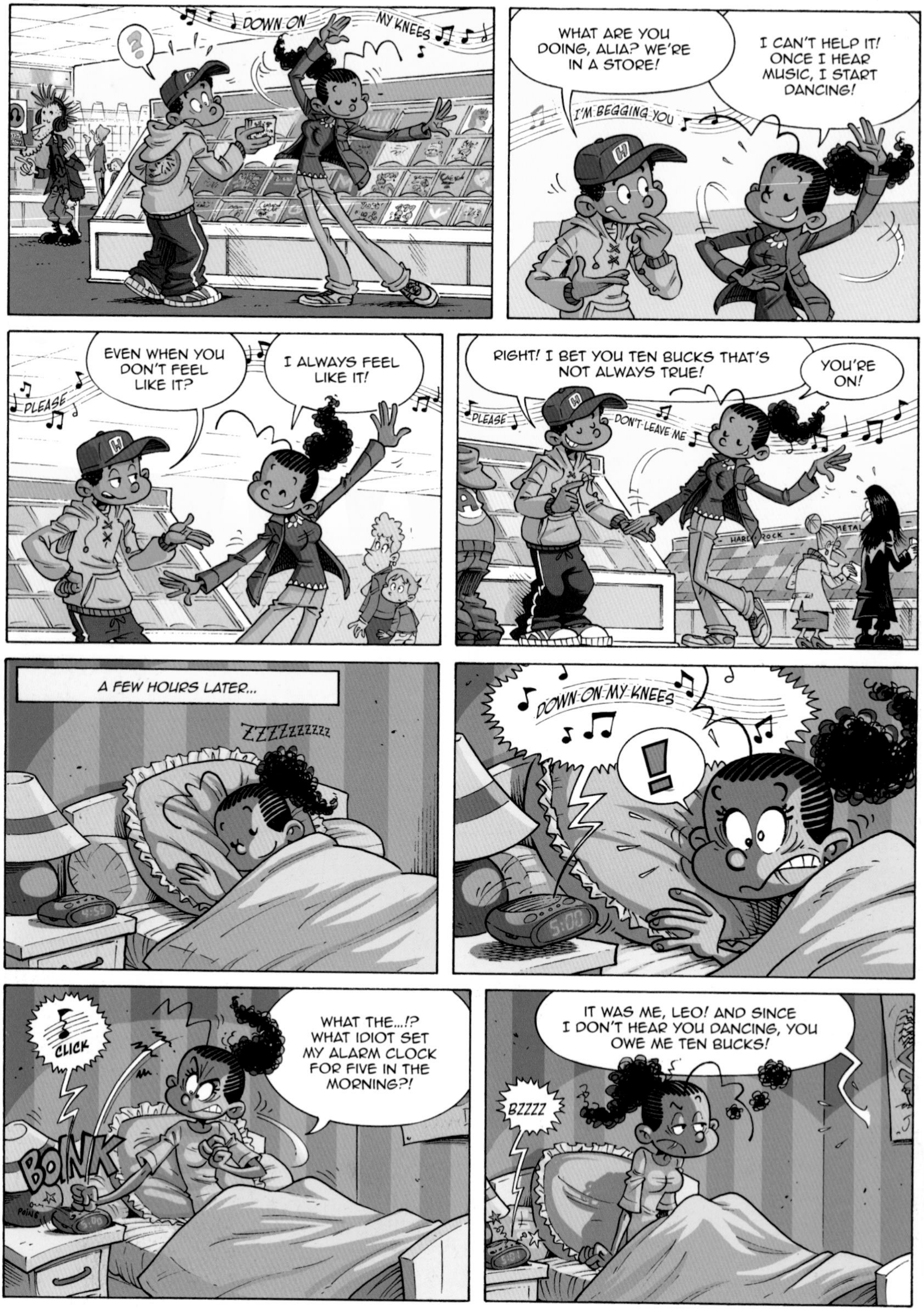
DOWN ON MY KNEES
?
WHAT ARE YOU DOING, ALIA? WE'RE IN A STORE!
I CAN'T HELP IT! ONCE I HEAR MUSIC, I START DANCING!
I'M BEGGING YOU
EVEN WHEN YOU DON'T FEEL LIKE IT?
I ALWAYS FEEL LIKE IT!
PLEASE
RIGHT! I BET YOU TEN BUCKS THAT'S NOT ALWAYS TRUE!
YOU'RE ON!
PLEASE
DON'T LEAVE ME
A FEW HOURS LATER...
ZZZZzzzzzz
DOWN ON MY KNEES
!
CLICK
BOINK
WHAT THE...!? WHAT IDIOT SET MY ALARM CLOCK FOR FIVE IN THE MORNING?!
BZZZZ
IT WAS ME, LEO! AND SINCE I DON'T HEAR YOU DANCING, YOU OWE ME TEN BUCKS!

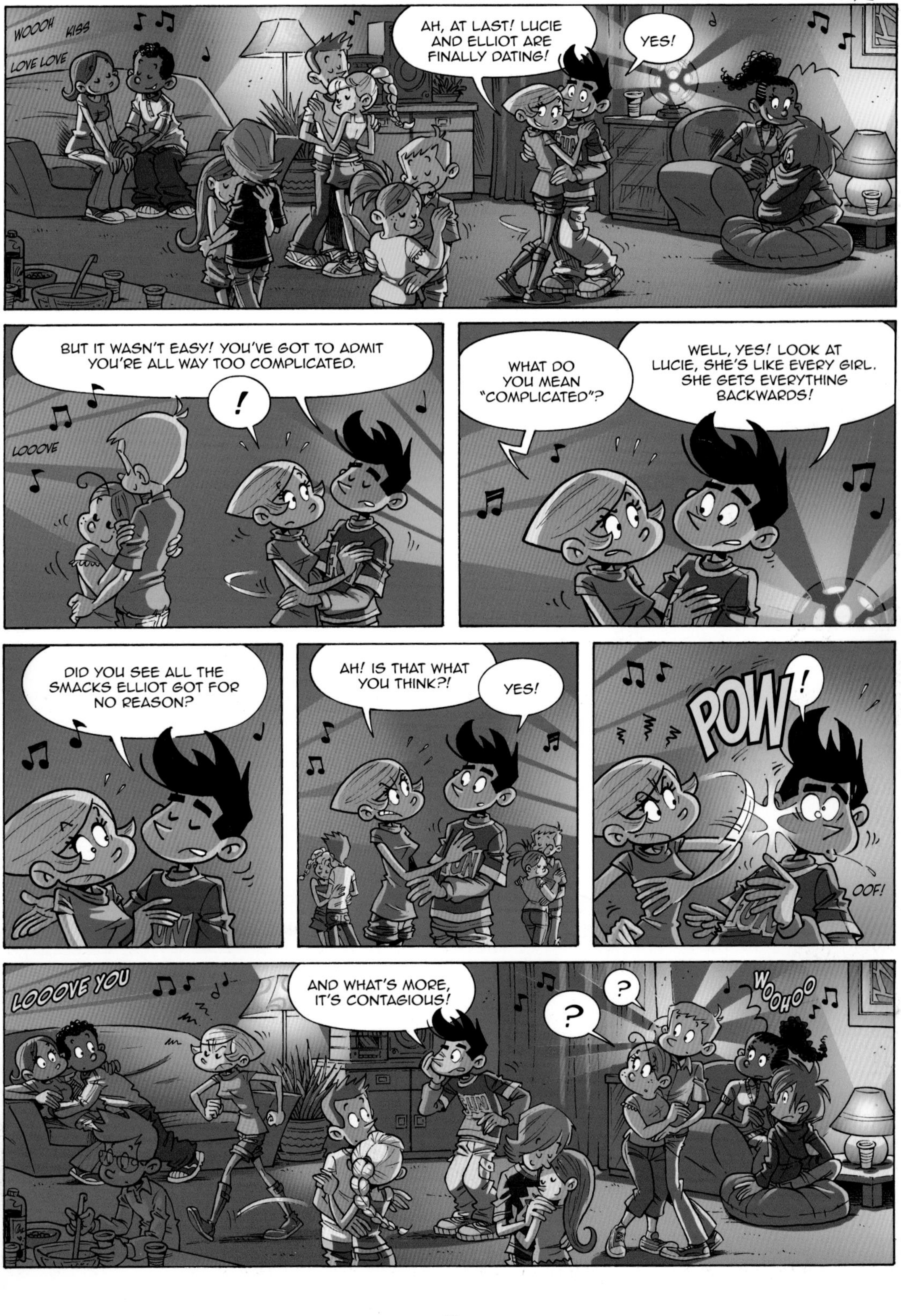
WOOOH
KISS
LOVE LOVE
AH, AT LAST! LUCIE AND ELLIOT ARE FINALLY DATING!
YES!
BUT IT WASN'T EASY! YOU'VE GOT TO ADMIT YOU'RE ALL WAY TOO COMPLICATED.
!
LOOOVE
WHAT DO YOU MEAN "COMPLICATED"?
WELL, YES! LOOK AT LUCIE, SHE'S LIKE EVERY GIRL. SHE GETS EVERYTHING BACKWARDS!
DID YOU SEE ALL THE SMACKS ELLIOT GOT FOR NO REASON?
AH! IS THAT WHAT YOU THINK?!
YES!
POW
!
OOF!
LOOOVE YOU
AND WHAT'S MORE, IT'S CONTAGIOUS!
?
?
WOOHOO

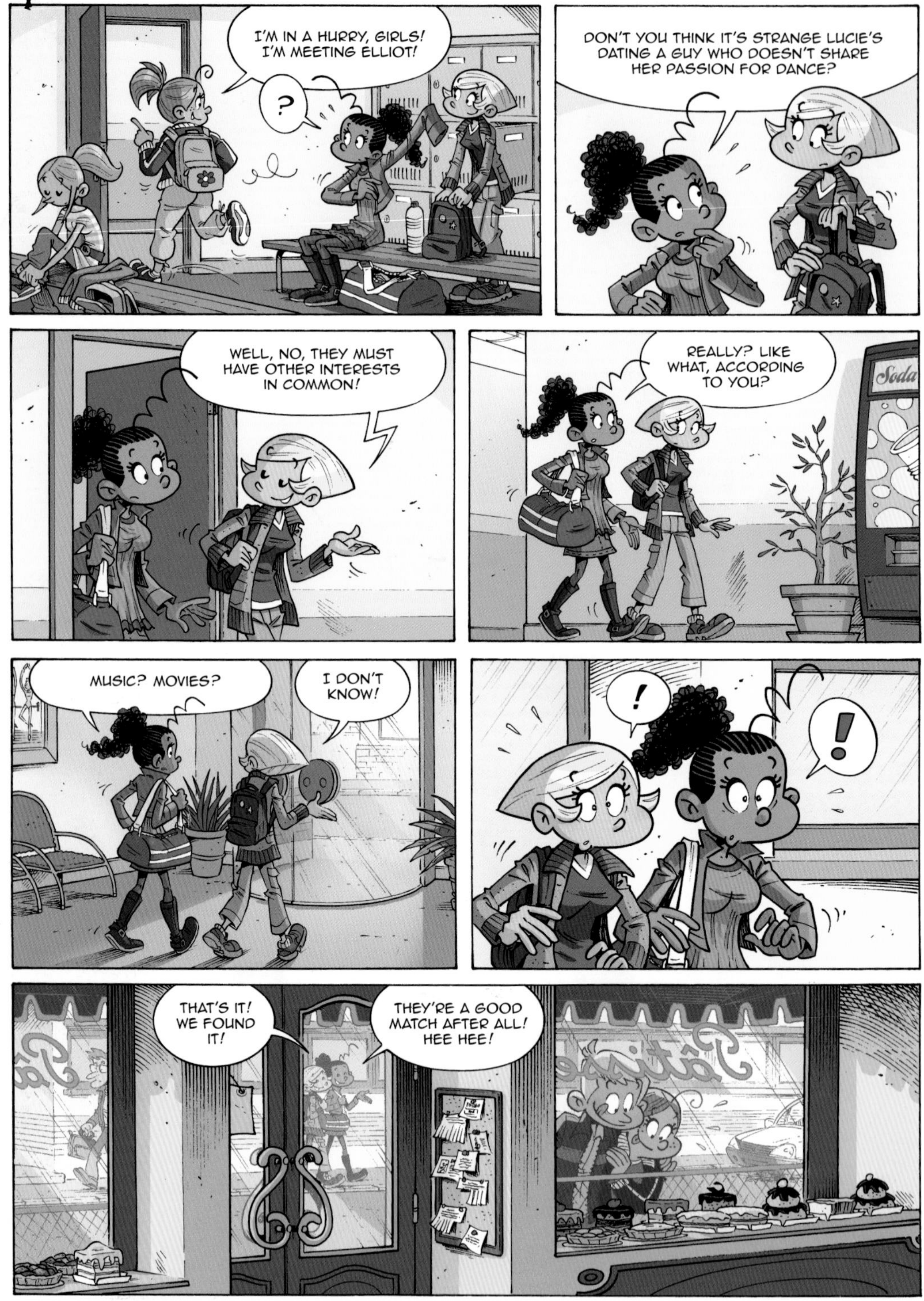
I'M IN A HURRY, GIRLS! I'M MEETING ELLIOT!
?
DON'T YOU THINK IT'S STRANGE LUCIE'S DATING A GUY WHO DOESN'T SHARE HER PASSION FOR DANCE?
WELL, NO, THEY MUST HAVE OTHER INTERESTS IN COMMON!
REALLY? LIKE WHAT, ACCORDING TO YOU?
Soda
MUSIC? MOVIES?
I DON'T KNOW!
!
!
THAT'S IT! WE FOUND IT!
THEY'RE A GOOD MATCH AFTER ALL! HEE HEE!

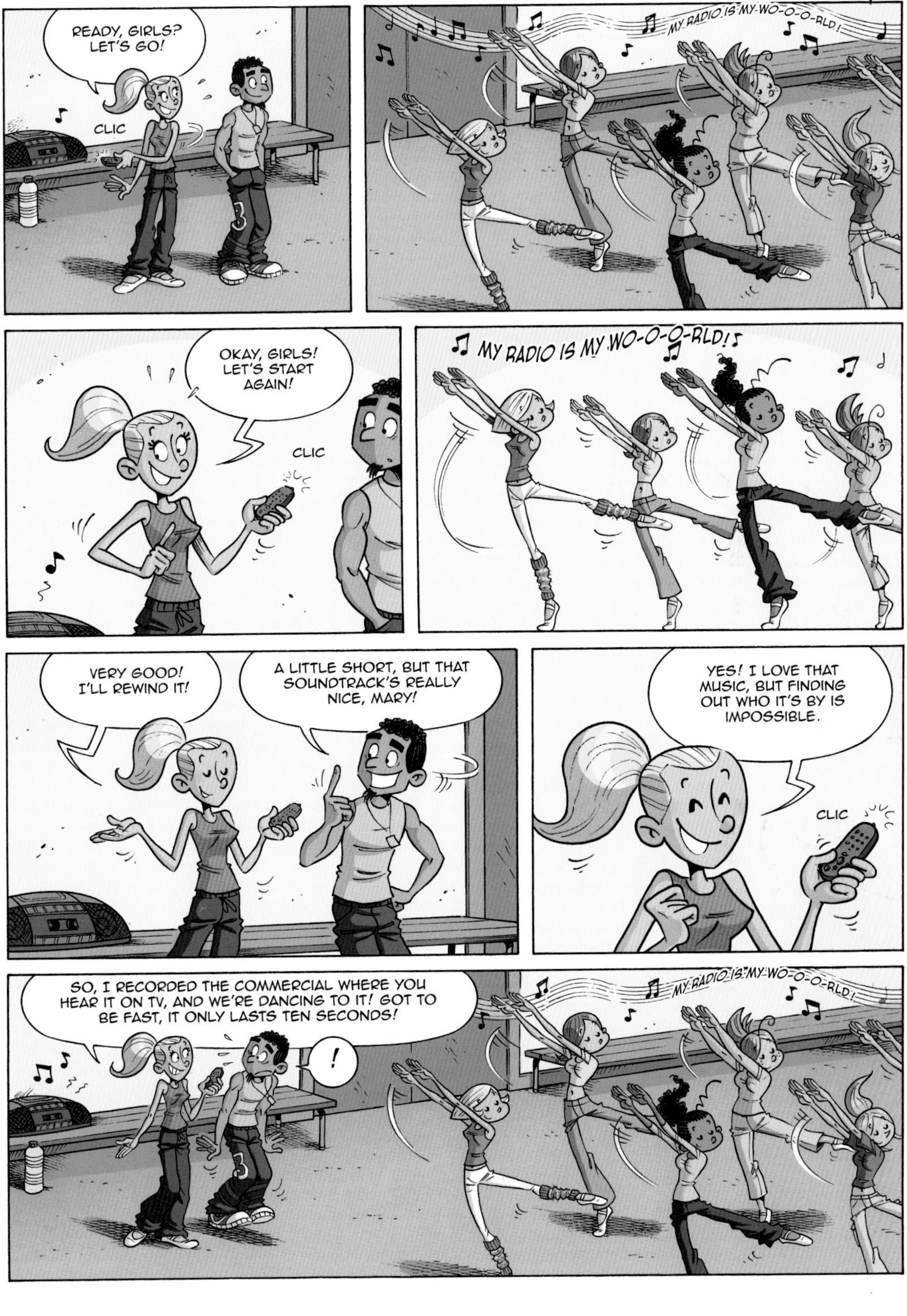
READY, GIRLS? LET'S GO!
CLIC
MY RADIO IS MY WO-O-O-RLD!
OKAY, GIRLS! LET'S START AGAIN!
CLIC
MY RADIO IS MY WO-O-O-RLD!
VERY GOOD! I'LL REWIND IT!
A LITTLE SHORT, BUT THAT SOUNDTRACK'S REALLY NICE, MARY!
YES! I LOVE THAT MUSIC, BUT FINDING OUT WHO IT'S BY IS IMPOSSIBLE.
CLIC
SO, I RECORDED THE COMMERCIAL WHERE YOU HEAR IT ON TV, AND WE'RE DANCING TO IT! GOT TO BE FAST, IT ONLY LASTS TEN SECONDS!
!
MY RADIO IS MY WO-O-O-RLD!

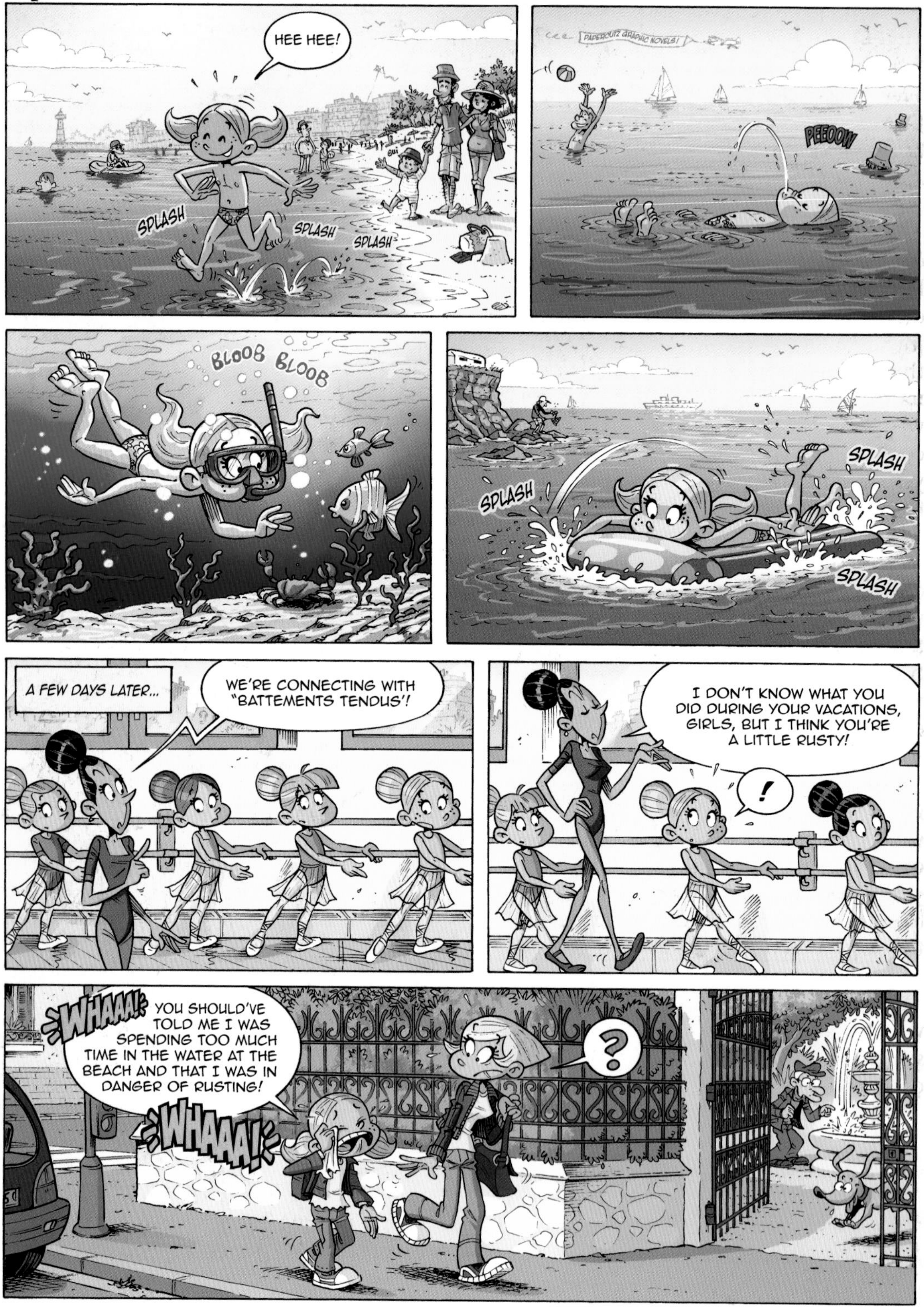
HEE HEE!
SPLASH
SPLASH
SPLASH
PAPERCUTZ GRAPHIC NOVELS!
PEEOOW
BLOOB BLOOB
SPLASH
SPLASH
SPLASH
A FEW DAYS LATER...
WE'RE CONNECTING WITH "BATTEMENTS TENDUS'!
I DON'T KNOW WHAT YOU DID DURING YOUR VACATIONS, GIRLS, BUT I THINK YOU'RE A LITTLE RUSTY!
!
WHAAA!
YOU SHOULD'VE TOLD ME I WAS SPENDING TOO MUCH TIME IN THE WATER AT THE BEACH AND THAT I WAS IN DANGER OF RUSTING!
WHAAA!
?

WATCH OUT FOR PAPERCUTZ™

Welcome to the foot-stomping fourth DANCE CLASS graphic novel by Crip & Béka. I'm Jim Salicrup, your Fox-Trotting Editor-in-Chief of Papercutz, the folks who dance to the beat of a different drummer and are dedicated to publishing great graphic novels for all ages. I'm here to talk a little bit about dancing...

Believe it or not, I've been taking dance lessons for years and years, and I've actually even learned a thing or two about dancing. Perhaps the most important lesson I've learned is that you shouldn't be afraid of dancing. Now, if you're already experiencing the joy of dancing, that may sound like the silliest thing you've ever heard. After all, few things are more fun than dancing. But, if you're someone who has never danced before, and wish you could, but are afraid to try because you think you may not be any good... I'm here to tell you, that you've got nothing to be afraid of!

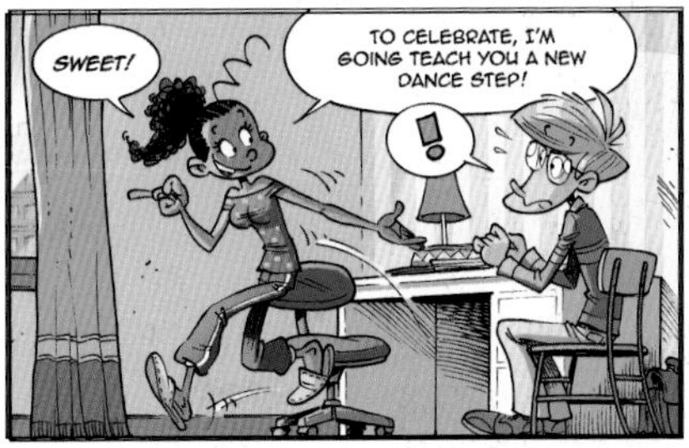
SWEET!
TO CELEBRATE, I'M GOING TEACH YOU A NEW DANCE STEP!
!

I know exactly how you feel. Despite my years of dance classes, I've never been what some would call a "natural born dancer." And that's totally okay with me, because my first passion has always been creating comicbooks. That's what I love to do, and that's what I get to do every day at Papercutz.

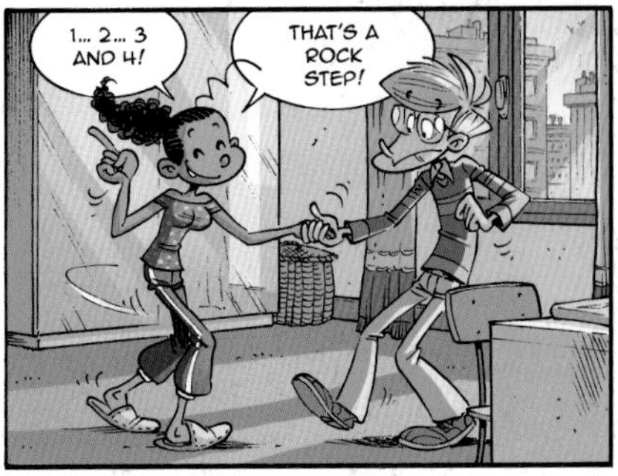
1... 2... 3 AND 4!
THAT'S A ROCK STEP!

Whenever you try something new, you need to get rid of any fear you might have of failure. You can't realistically expect to do anything perfectly on your very first attempt. Just relax, and give it your best shot, and I promise that no one will laugh at you. Everyone had to start at the beginning, and they usually remember how scared they were too. Dancers tend to want to see more people dancing, and are usually willing to be very supportive.

You should also ask yourself, what do you have to be afraid of? Is it the end of the world if you're not the best dancer who ever lived? If you're interested in dancing, it's something you should do for only one reason—you want to dance. So, just get up and dance! You'll never regret it!

Thanks,

Jim

STAY IN TOUCH!

EMAIL: salicrup@papercutz.com
WEB: www.papercutz.com
TWITTER: @papercutzgn
FACEBOOK: PAPERCUTZGRAPHICNOVELS
BIRTHDAY CARDS: Papercutz, 160 Broadway, Suite 700, East Wing, New York, NY 10038

More Great Graphic Novels from PAPERCUTZ™

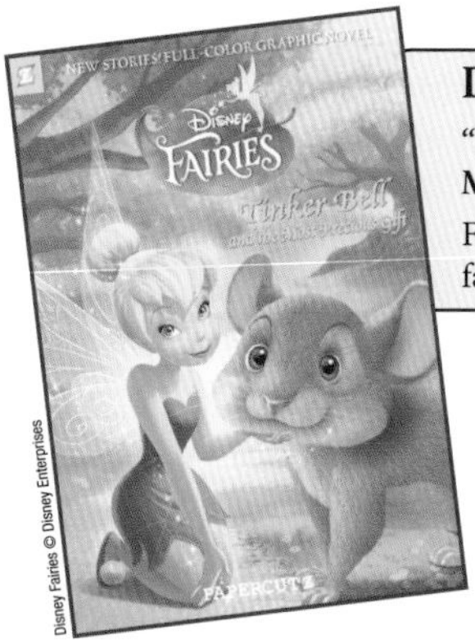

Disney FAIRIES
Tinker Bell
PAPERCUTZ

DISNEY FAIRIES #11
"Tinker Bell and the Most Precious Gift"

Four magical tales featuring the fairies from Pixie Hollow!

ERNEST & REBECCA #4
"The Land of Walking Stones"

A 6 ½ year old girl and her microbial buddy against the world!

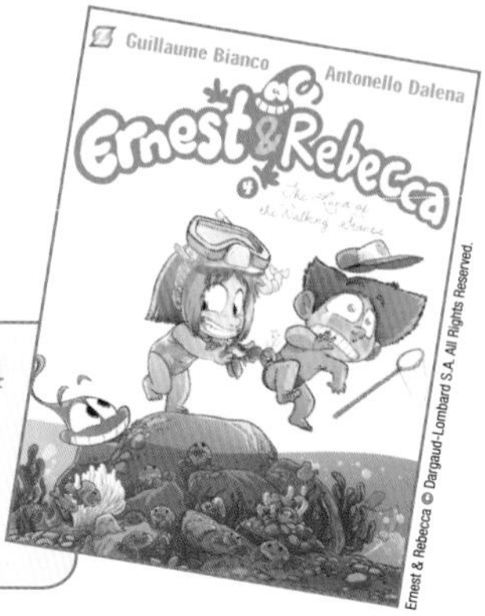

Guillaume Bianco
Antonello Dalena
Ernest & Rebecca

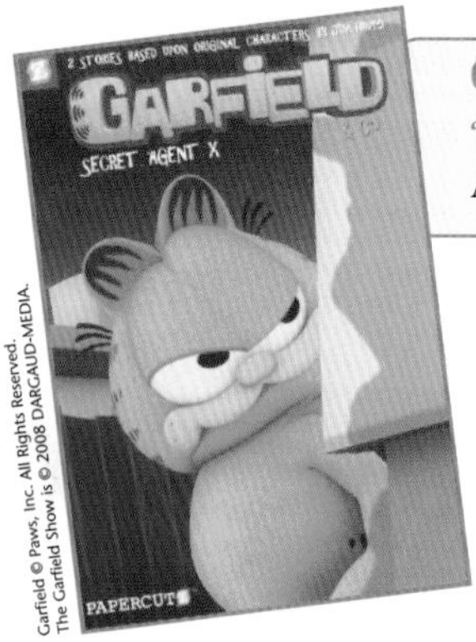

GARFIELD
SECRET AGENT X
PAPERCUTZ

GARFIELD & Co #8
"Secret Agent X"

As seen on the Cartoon Network!

MONSTER #4
"Monster Turkey"

The almost normal adventures of an almost ordinary family... with a pet monster!

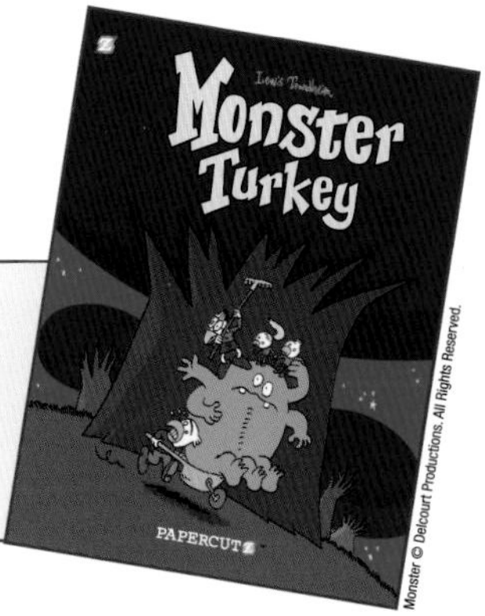

Monster Turkey
PAPERCUTZ

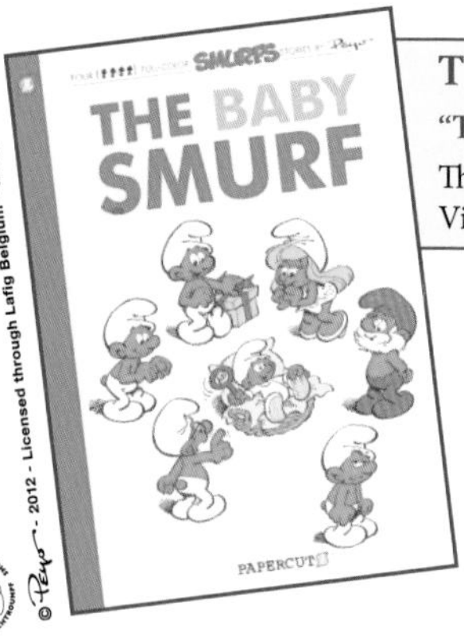

SMURFS
THE BABY SMURF
PAPERCUTZ

THE SMURFS #14
"The Baby Smurf"

There's a new arrival in the Smurfs Village!

SYBIL THE BACKPACK FAIRY #3
"Aithor"

What's cooler than a fairy in your backpack? How about a flying horse?!

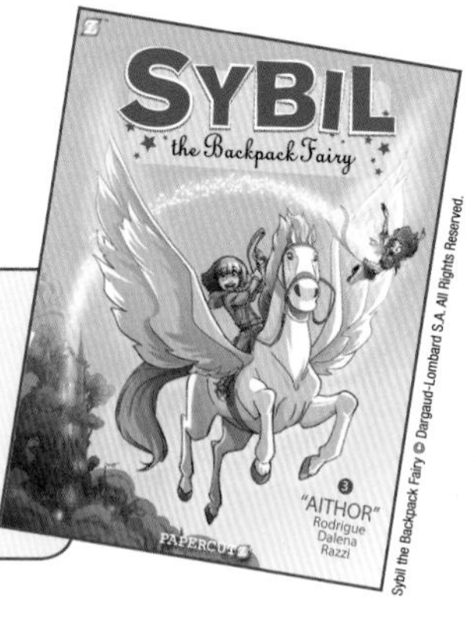

SYBIL
the Backpack Fairy
"AITHOR"
Rodrigue
Dalena
Razzi
PAPERCUTZ

Available at better booksellers everywhere!

Or order directly from us! DISNEY FAIRIES is available in paperback for $7.99, in hardcover for $11.99; ERNEST & REBECCA is $11.99 in hardcover only; GARFIELD & Co is available in hardcover only for $7.99; MONSTER is available in hardcover only for $9.99; THE SMURFS are available in paperback for $5.99, in hardcover for $10.99; and SYBIL THE BACKPACK FAIRY is available in hardcover only for $11.99.

Please add $4.00 for postage and handling for the first book, add $1.00 for each additional book.

Please make check payable to NBM Publishing Send to: PAPERCUTZ,160 Broadway, Suite 700, East Wing, New York, NY 10038

(1-800-886-1223)

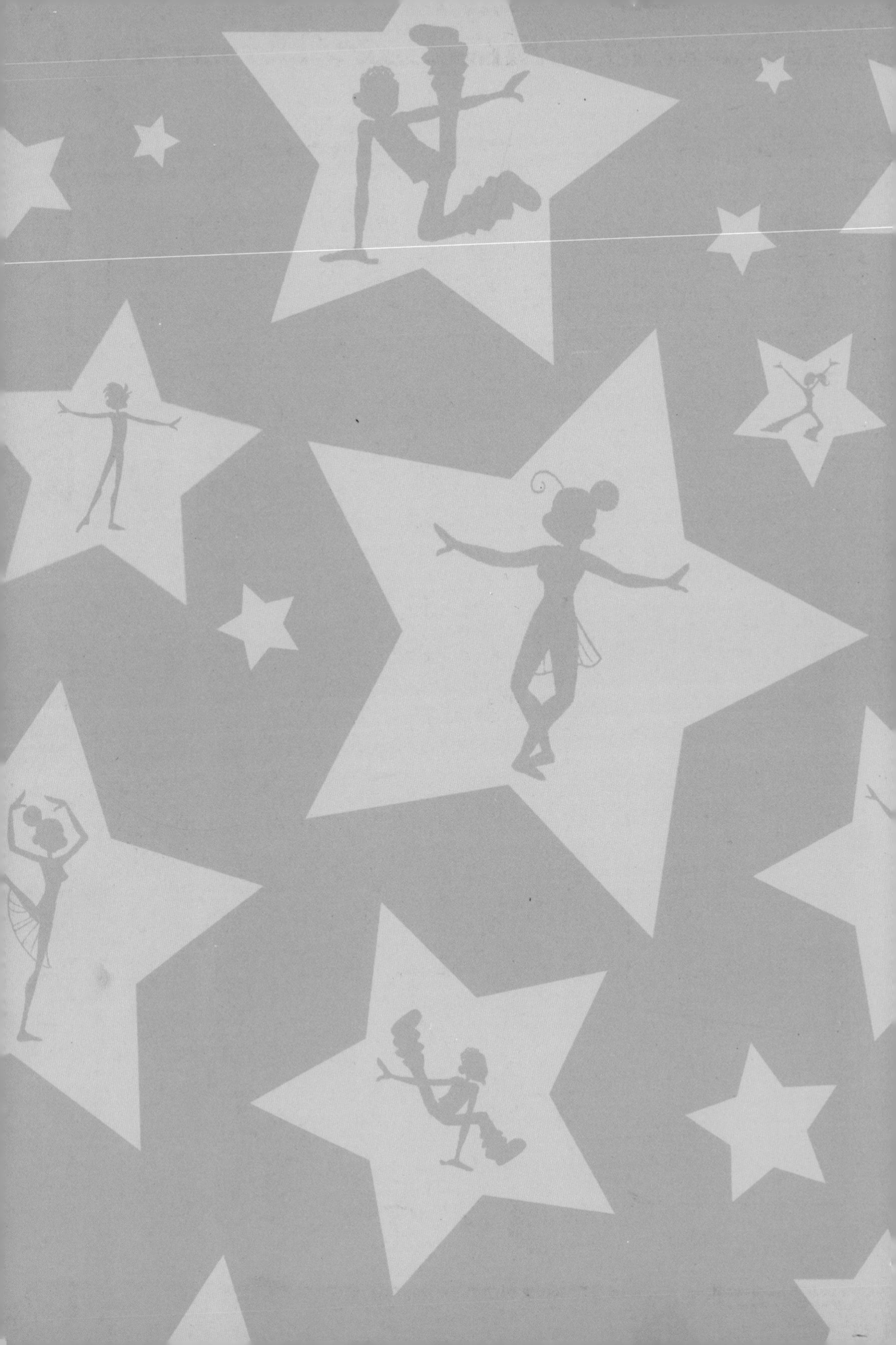